THE DONATION MAN

Judy Snider

World Castle Publishing, LLC
Pensacola, Florida
Copyright © Judy Snider 2017
Paperback ISBN: 9781629897967
eBook ISBN: 9781629897974
First Edition World Castle Publishing, LLC, September 18, 2017
http://www.worldcastlepublishing.com
Licensing Notes
Cover: Karen Fuller
Photo: Judy Snider
Editor: Maxine Bringenberg

Reggie did not know where she was, but she felt a tear roll down her cheek as the realization she might not escape from this nightmare set in. There were so many things she wanted to tell her parents and Sam. Another tear rolled down her cheek. She thought about Lucy, and who would take care of her when she was gone. Then a voice whispered to her, "You must fight!"

CHAPTER 1

Reggie woke up with one of the killer headaches she only got if she skipped her coffee for a day. Instead of slowly getting out of bed, she gently pushed her cat Lucy aside, rolled out of bed, and hurried to use the bathroom. She went into the kitchen and grabbed the bag of espresso to start a pot of coffee she certainly intended to drink all by herself.

Next, she grabbed a glass of pineapple juice and slathered some peanut butter on bread for her breakfast. She went outside her apartment door and got the paper. There was something about a paper in hand and a cup of coffee that was more satisfying to her in the morning than going to her phone or computer to get the news like she did the rest of the day. She avoided the television news because she was a television reporter, and found herself critiquing the reports and feeling as if she was doing work. She sat at her kitchen table, sipped her coffee, and ate breakfast in silence, because even the sound of the birds outside made her head ache. Not a very exciting morning for a newswoman.

When she traveled on special assignment, she started her morning with the hotel's brunch and enjoyed having someone pour rich dark coffee into her cup. That was why she'd skipped her coffee yesterday; she had to show someone around town in the early morning. She forgot her usual coffee and took them instead to the local sights. They'd stopped in the park to listen to jazz and drink a mint julep and a Hurricane. Yes, maybe her headache was partly due to the drinks, as she was not a big drinker, but she always drank more when showing someone around. She laughed to herself. *I am such a wild woman.*

Of course, since living in New Orleans, she'd taken them for coffee and the powdered sugar donut like beignets by Jackson Square. It was such a hot day that she ordered some chocolate milk to quench her thirst. It was the middle of summer in New Orleans, and she called it the three shower season, where you needed three showers a day just to try to keep cool. She had lived in Virginia and Washington D.C., but she still found the summers in New Orleans to be the season she wished she was out of town for.

She had been in New Orleans for three months

on a special assignment. Some people did not like the city, but Reggie found the people to be warm and wonderful, and the food the best in the United States. She found a good sublet on the trolley line uptown by Carrolton Avenue, and its location made it easy to get to all her assignments. Sam, the love of her life, was in Virginia and would visit, but had no desire to stay in New Orleans. As much as Reggie loved him, there was something about the city and people here that made her never want to leave. Lately, this had been the topic of their conversations that left both Sam and Reggie at an impasse in their relationship.

Besides, Reggie felt she was just beginning to really feel safe going outside after being shot last year. Her shrink helped her a lot in New Orleans, but even the sound of a car backfiring could send her into a post-traumatic panic. She looked down at the scar and felt thankful she was even alive.

Reggie sighed, forcing herself to enjoy her breakfast and read the paper instead of analyzing her relationship with Sam or thinking about how they both were almost killed. Plus, it made her headache ten times worse. *Let's add a little tension headache to my caffeine withdrawal and a slight hangover.* She laughed to herself.

Her favorite Elvis song began to play on her ringing cell phone. She winced and turned down the volume.

"Hello."

"Hello, may I please speak to Reggie Page?"

"Speaking."

The deep voice on the other end said, "I wanted to say thank you for the help you have given to my foundation in the past. I was wondering if we can count on your help again?"

Reggie liked to give to many organizations, but after hearing from some over and over, she kept a little pink book listing who she made a contribution to, the date, and the amount. Usually, Reggie would get the book, but this morning she was too beat and pleasantly said, "I'm sorry, sir, but I will not be donating. Could you please tell me one more time the name of the organization you represent?" The man said the name of the organization, but Reggie couldn't remember donating to it before. She again said, "I won't be donating at this time."

"How about if I sign you up for our lowest amount? Anything helps," he asked.

"No, but I may give next year. Please call me in a year." She wanted to say, *don't call me when I have been out partying late, and my head is foggy.*

Instead of saying fine and agreeing to call in a year, the man grew increasingly cool on the phone. "I know you can donate something. Just think of all the people you can help. I will send you out this packet in the mail today."

"No," Reggie said firmly. "I appreciate all you do to help people, and I may give next year, but not now."

"I am sorry, ma'am, but you must give today. If you don't, people will be in need because of you! We all have to give in life, or it will come back to haunt us," he murmured.

Reggie could not believe what she was hearing. This person was way out of line, and she needed to end the conversation. "I am going to hang up now. Try me next year, goodbye."

Reggie hung up the phone. Her head throbbed even harder now. She had always been assertive, but in cases like this, she realized the person was only doing their job, and she was nice to them. It annoyed her to get someone who was trying to make her feel guilty.

Suddenly her phone rang. She answered it, not bothering to see who it was.

"Hello, Reggie here."

The man with the deep voice said, "I am sorry we got cut off. I bet you were just ready to donate to our organization."

Reggie was starting to feel a little uneasy now. "No, I told you I was not donating."

9

"I know you didn't mean that," the man said, sounding very sure of himself and trying to sound as pleasant as possible. "I know you want to help all the people who need it, and I bet you have changed your mind."

"I have not changed my mind, and I want you to not call me again. In fact, please take my name off your list."

"I can't do that, ma'am!"

"Oh, yes you can. Please do. I am hanging up again."

"Fine, I will put you down for ten dollars, our lowest amount, and we will send the packet in the mail."

"No, no," Reggie said, her voice raising. "I do not want to donate!"

There was a long silence on the phone, and then the man said, "If you don't donate, my job is on the line."

"I am truly sorry, but I am not donating," Reggie said, and hung up.

Reggie took a sip of coffee. What he'd said did pull at Reggie's heartstrings a little. If he had not given her such a guilt trip, maybe she would have changed her mind. *Oh, stop it, Reggie, you can't help everyone.*

She started to worry what if he did lose his job

when the phone rang again.

"Reggie here," she said, not thinking the same man would dare call again.

The man was on the phone again, this time speaking in almost a whisper. "I know you want to donate. I will call you tomorrow when you're in a better mood. We all have to give in life, and if we don't, it always comes back to haunt us."

There was silence followed by a soft click.

Chapter 2

What the man on the phone did not realize was her boyfriend was a cop in Virginia, and The Donation Man, as she was now referring to him, had better not mess with her, or she would have Sam get him.

She started to think about the man who'd almost killed her in Virginia. If it had not been for Sam, his partner Mike, and her friend Maggie, who she'd met while they were being hunted by The Bomber, she would be dead. She did have some nightmares about The Bomber, and although he was dead, something in this guy's tone made her feel uneasy.

Last year was a whole other story she didn't want to start thinking about today. Besides, she'd seen a shrink for a while, and it helped. Not too many shrinks were surprised if their patient had nightmares when they were almost killed.

She started dating Sam after that, and it seemed

like he had been in her life forever. This long distance romance was a pain, but she preferred it over not seeing Sam. Just the thought of him made her start to long for him and his caress.

Maggie remained a good friend of hers, and had fallen in love with Sam's partner, Mike. She missed all three of them, but started making a few friends in New Orleans on the weekends she did not fly back to Virginia.

Reggie had accepted the assignment in New Orleans to help with a documentary being done on the city, which included its history, food, Katrina, and so much more that the assignment was for six months. Three months down and three more to go. She had been here years ago and was enchanted by the city and people then, and in love with the food. When her producer mentioned it to her, thinking she would turn it down since she was seeing Sam, she said, "Yes, of course I will go. But can I get funds to fly back to Virginia every once in a while?"

That night, three months ago, over a glass of wine, she'd told Sam what she was going to do. He'd felt betrayed because she'd made the decision without even talking to him. He wanted her to be independent and take the job, but she knew he was hurt. Reggie did feel she was a little selfish in not talking to him, and promised him she would discuss things with him in the future.

To lighten the mood, Reggie grabbed her tablet and cuddled closer on the couch. She showed him the places they could see and where they could eat. Sam laughed and said, "Is food all you ever think about?"

"In New Orleans, of course. But here there are other things on my mind," she replied. "Gosh, I wonder what they could be?" She turned towards Sam and hungrily kissed his lips, running her hands through his hair. Sam pulled her closer and began kissing her neck gently, slowly unbuttoning her blouse all the while. He kissed her lips hungrily with kisses that took both their breaths away. He gently pulled her shirt off and her cami over her head.

"Let me see you naked," she whispered into his ear." They both started pulling off each other's clothes and felt the heat of the moment take over. Their passion rose as if their bodies were on fire, hotter and hotter until they both moaned in ecstasy. They laid in each other's arms, content at actually being in love.

CHAPTER 3

Putting the caller out of her mind, Reggie dressed and headed to the television station. Today she was filming an interview with a group of the top chefs in New Orleans. Many of them had been in the restaurant business for years, and had passed on the love of owning a restaurant to their families. They agreed to let Reggie and Jane come to their restaurants and film. During and after Katrina, the proud people of New Orleans had pulled together to keep their businesses going, and many restaurants stayed open to show their support of the city.

It was hard to narrow it down to a few restaurant chefs for the interview, because they were all so good. It was now down to five restaurants. She decided to do the restaurants in the French Quarter itself, but she would have loved to mention the fantastic roasted oysters at Drago's near Bourbon Street, as well as the

Commander's Palace brunch, and too many other places in and outside the Quarter she ate at. An easy five pounds she had put on, but they were worth every bite.

Her camera woman, Jane, was really talented and also not afraid to give Reggie pointers on the history of the city, directions, politics, etc. Jane was a native, had survived Katrina, and made the perfect match when doing a documentary. Jane had an *in* with many of the people in the city, which made it easier to set up interviews.

Reggie met Jane in the Quarter, as she now called it, and they went to the first restaurant to start the interview. This was a lovely restaurant with a garden setting and a fountain. The chef and owner greeted them both warmly, let them film the restaurant, showed how they made bananas Foster, a famous New Orleans dish, and sat down to talk about their restaurant and life in New Orleans.

As a reporter, Reggie could tell early on if this was going to be a good interview and if the public would like it, or if she would have to pull every sentence out of who she was interviewing. This one was easy, and the chef and owner a delight. Of course, it did not hurt that as part of the interview both she and Jane got to sample the bananas Foster. The rest of the day went pretty much the same. Each restaurant seemed to want to delight her the most, and she ate and laughed more than she had done in a long time. She even planned to write a thank you note to thank each restaurant for their time and hospitality.

Just as they stepped out of the last restaurant around 5 p.m., Reggie's phone rang. *Must be Sam,* Reggie thought, not looking at the number.

"Hello, Reggie here," she said automatically.

"Hello, Reggie. I hope you're having a good day. I wanted to call back and see how much you would like to donate to our organization we spoke about this morning," the deep familiar voice almost purred into the phone.

Reggie froze. *What the hell?* she thought.

"I asked you not to call anymore, sir, as I won't be donating anything 'till next year," Reggie said, not having time to get an angry tone.

"I knew you would change your mind, so I called back. Am I putting you down for those ten dollars I mentioned this morning? I know we can count on you!"

"Again, sir, do not call me again. Take my name off the list, and if you call again, I will talk to your supervisor."

There was silence, then the man repeated his same speech, ignoring what Reggie had just said. "I know you want to donate. We all have to give in life, and if we don't, it always comes back to haunt us."

Reggie felt her face getting flushed and blood pressure rising. "That's it! Please let me talk to your supervisor!"

"You're right. That is it for now," he said smoothly into the phone. "My supervisor is busy currently. Talk to you again soon."

Reggie just stared at the phone for a while. "What...? But...."

Jane stared at Reggie now. "You look like you have seen a ghost. What is going on?"

"Oh, some donation place bugged me this morning about giving money, and the guy was really persistent. Way out of line. I told him to take my name off the list, and he called me again. What is weird is he is so pleasant and upbeat. Yet, there was this pushiness. Gives me the creeps, Jane."

Jane looked at Reggie. "I have been in this business long enough to know that there are lots of crazy people out there. The monsters aren't in the movies but in real life. If this guy keeps bugging you, you need to tell someone." She then frowned at Reggie.

"I am going to tell Sam, but in the meantime, it just has shaken me a little. Who would have thought one call could get me nervous? Me, Reggie, the reporter." She laughed with less than her usual loud, infectious laugh. "Jane, tomorrow we meet at ten at the Mardi

Gras World Museum to add that interview for the show." She had heard it was a perfect place for locals, and was excited to tour it herself. Besides, hearing about all the Mardi Gras floats, she also found out they had plastic animals, characters, etc. they make for amusement parks, along with places in the USA and internationally. It was by the conference center downtown, so it was easy to get to.

Jane lived uptown by campus, so sometimes if they did not have too much equipment, Reggie would hop on the streetcar by her apartment and ride with her downtown after Jane got on at her stop. Jane had regular use of one of the station's SUV's since she was always on assignment for them.

Jane sometimes asked Reggie if Ben, her twelve-year-old son, could watch the interviews, as he too wanted to be a camera person or television reporter when he got older. He was a really nice kid, and Jane was a great mom. Reggie laughed when Jane would ruffle his hair and give him some mom advice. Jeff, Jane's husband, owned a store in one of the tourists' sections of the city, and always had some cool New Orleans shirt on when Reggie saw him. If they were on a shoot near the store, Jane stopped in to bring him a cup of coffee or get him a po' boy sandwich if he had not packed lunch.

"Are you going to stay downtown, Reggie, or do

you want a ride back in the station's SUV?"

"I think I will go home, just chill, and watch some comedy or read a book. Besides, Lucy hasn't seen me since morning, so she will snuggle next to me all night or bug me to feed her. Plus, it has been awhile since I had lots of time to Skype with Sam, and I miss seeing him!"

"Sometime this week, come on over, and my guys can make you laugh with all the stories of their week. Even at twelve, Ben is learning how to cook like his dad, so you're in for a treat!"

Reggie laughed. She knew Jane loved to eat and her husband loved to cook. They were a match made in heaven. It warmed Reggie's heart that she and Jane had gotten so close. Reggie was a good cook, but she liked *not* having to cook. Besides, in New Orleans, to stop at her little local dive and take home some red beans and rice on a Monday was her idea of a great meal. Of course, adding a New Orleans beer topped her meal off.

CHAPTER 4

Reggie changed into her jeans and poured herself a glass of beer. She tore off a chunk of French bread and stuck it on top of her plate loaded with red beans and rice, then put a small dish of Lucy's food on the floor and laughed. People would certainly think she was a cat lady who had dinner with and talked to her cat during dinner. Reggie didn't mind. She loved Lucy being around.

She grabbed a few magazines and was reading them after dinner when her phone rang. She picked it up, thinking, *Why is it that whenever I am eating, people seem to call?*

This call she did not mind at all...it was Sam. Sometimes he called when she was having dinner and asked her to do an online chat so they could have dinner together. He was so sweet. At times, he even put flowers on his table and said, "If you were

21

here, they would be for you." He was an excellent cook, so sometimes as she threw together something for dinner, he would have the most tempting meals and chuckle as she tried to be funny and grab them through the screen.

"Hi, Sam."

"Hi, Reggie. Do you want to go online or is this okay?"

"Let's talk by phone because as I am eating, Lucy is pressed up to me on the couch, and you know how perturbed she gets when I disturb her by going to the computer. I would love to see your gorgeous face, but I will just pretend you're here." She laughed.

"So, how was your day?" Sam asked.

"It was incredible! Jane and I got to interview about five of the great restaurants in the Quarter, and it was interesting hearing the history of the restaurants and their owners. The owners were very kind and funny, so I think it will be a significant part of the documentary."

"What wonderful things did you eat?" Sam chuckled. Reggie loved to tell him more about the interviews she'd done, so he just listened as she told him all the details. Reggie also was the talkative one in the relationship. Sam enjoyed her zest and enthusiasm for everything.

Once Reggie told Sam all the details of her

interview, she asked him, "How was your day?" She had left out the part about the caller. *That can wait until later in the conversation,* she thought. *After we catch up.*

"Not too bad. You know in this town, we don't have too many big crimes since our brush with the illegal animal trade, thank goodness. I did have someone shoplifting at several locations. We think it's the same person, but can't be sure. They were during my duty, so I am checking them out. We may have a kid take something, but we've never gotten a string of them all happening in the space of two hours.

"Otherwise not much new. Big picnic happening in small town USA, and I can't wait to see you in two weekends! There are a few movies coming out I may take myself to that probably wouldn't interest you."

"Sam...you know I needed to take this job," Reggie said, hearing the very slight *if you hadn't left* tone that had crept into Sam's voice.

"I know, Reggie. I really do. But occasionally it upsets me you're so far away. I know the job is ideal for you, and we do see each other. I just guess I wanted to pout a little. It was a long day. I need to finish this good meal, finish my beer, and dream of you."

"You could write me a love letter, Sam," Reggie

laughed. With all the e-mails and texts, she would enjoy a romantic handwritten letter from Sam she could hold in her hands.

"So everything is fine?"

Reggie hesitated to tell Sam about the caller. It had made her uncomfortable enough that she did not know if she wanted Sam to know about it. But she knew he would want to know. "Some donation place bugged me this morning about giving money, and the guy was really persistent. I told him to take my name off the list, and he called me again."

"This guy probably has to meet a quota for his job, and that is why he may be pushy. What organization did he say he was from and where?" asked Sam.

Reggie thought hard but could not remember the name or what city it was in. "I will have to ask if he calls again. Sam, there is something about this guy that just gives me the creeps. I don't know if it is his voice or the fact he was nice. I just don't know."

"Try not to aggravate the guy next time if he calls. He might just have been having a bad day. If you have any more problems, which you probably won't, let me know," Sam said.

"You're probably right, Sam. I will be just another person who said no to him tomorrow, and it will be over." Reggie took a deep breath and relaxed into the couch. "Love you, Sam. You have a good week, and

I can't wait to see you soon."

"Love you too, Reggie. Goodnight."

Reggie gathered up her dishes and took them into the kitchen. Living in a camelback house gave her an appreciation for the beautiful old places of New Orleans. When she first came to New Orleans, and someone asked her if she wanted to be in a camelback near campus, Reggie was totally confused. The real estate agent must have seen the look on her face and chuckled because of it. "What I mean is, do you want to live in a house that is divided in two with each side being a mirror image of the other? The two upstairs bedrooms sit at the back of the house and look like the hump of a camel."

"Sure, that would be an enjoyable experience for me. But if it's too expensive, the station won't cover it," Reggie said.

"No, actually, this place is very reasonable. The owner lives on the next block and usually rents it to students or young professionals, so you fit the bill. Besides, the woman who lives in the other half is a real nice person and won't be having too many loud parties."

"Well, I hope she doesn't think I am a downer. Maybe a party or two is what I need. After all, I will be living in New Orleans," Reggie responded.

Annie, her neighbor, was a vet tech at a local

clinic, and was nice as well as fun. They had gone out for a drink a few times, and shared a pizza off and on at each other's place. Annie was looking for the man of her dreams, but had not found him yet.

As Reggie thought about all that had happened to her in the past three months, she washed her dishes and then changed into her robe. Tonight she was glad her blinds were tightly closed, and she put her alarm on. She couldn't settle in once dark came unless all the blinds were closed. She had watched so many movies in life, and having survived The Bomber, she felt nervous that someone could look in and see if she was alone.

Reggie still couldn't shake the calls she'd gotten today and the man's voice, so she grabbed her baseball bat and put it under the bed. She would be embarrassed to tell Sam she did that, but it made her feel safe. She did know how to use a gun, but she still couldn't bring herself to own one considering the past.

Reggie got into bed, tossed and turned for only a few minutes, and then drifted off into a deep sleep.

CHAPTER 5

Something woke Reggie up, covered in sweat and a little disoriented. She looked at the clock...3 a.m. Suddenly, she heard the agitated barking of the neighbor's dog, followed by the sound of heavy footsteps near the front of the house. Her heart racing, Reggie slipped out of bed, put on her robe, and grabbed her baseball bat. Heading softly down the stairs, she crossed the kitchen and started towards the front of the house, part of her afraid to go anywhere near the front door. All she heard were the cats fighting and dogs barking. There was no other sound. Everything looked okay.

Reggie turned to head back upstairs. Suddenly, there was a loud knocking at the door. Turning her head towards the door, she saw a shadow through the curtains covering the glass on the door and froze. She was ready to run when she heard a voice.

"Reggie! Reggie! It's me, Annie. I heard you screaming and ran over. Are you all right?"

Thank God, Reggie thought, and went to open the door.

Annie stood looking just as afraid as Reggie. She gave Annie a big hug. "I just had a nightmare. I'm so sorry I woke you up. I didn't even realize I screamed. Let's talk tomorrow."

"Are you sure, Reggie?" Annie asked.

"Yes, go. Thanks for coming over."

"See you tomorrow." As she began to turn around, she turned back and said, "You know, Reggie, since your bedroom is on the other side of mine and the walls are thin, we should have some signal like pounding the wall that you're okay or I am okay."

"Great idea. And how about one that says it is just Sam and me having a good time, or if you're with someone?" Reggie laughed.

"One track mind. Goodnight, Reggie." Annie laughed as she started to walk back home.

Reggie went back upstairs after grabbing a glass of orange juice and started to fall into another deep sleep. As she lay there, she thought to herself, *But whose footsteps were those?*

CHAPTER 6

"Oh, shit," she moaned as her alarm screamed in her ear the next morning. "I am not ready to get up." She still had her robe on from last night, and quickly made a cup of coffee, grabbed a banana, and wolfed it down before taking her shower. Reggie needed to be awake and alert for the interview at Mardi Gras World today. She had promised to be on time; Jane was always on time, and Reggie tried but found it so hard.

She did the best she could in getting herself ready considering her sleepless night. When she looked into her mirror, she saw her skin looked unlined today, and her green eyes sparkled, probably due to the strong coffee she'd guzzled down. She wore her long dark hair in a ponytail, and put eye shadow and lipstick on without having to use a makeup artist.

Looking in the mirror, she was dressed and ready

to go. Reggie gave herself her usual thumbs up sign and headed downstairs. Jane was going to pick her up in about ten minutes. The walk from the trolley was not too far, but today, Reggie needed to not look wilted.

As she put her coffee cup in the sink, her phone rang.

Must be Jane asking if I'm ready, she thought. This was something she did every time she was going to pick Reggie up. "Hi, Jane. Yes, I am ready!"

There was a slight pause, and a man's voice said, "Good, I would like to see you ready." A small laugh followed.

Reggie knew who it was but asked, "Who is this?" trying to keep an even tone in her voice.

"Why, Reggie, you don't remember me? I am calling today to give you another chance to donate to our organization. I have the ten-dollar packet right here to send out to you today."

"I am not donating, and do not call again!" Reggie found herself more and more annoyed as she hung up.

The phone rang again.

Reggie didn't answer it after checking the number. It rang again and again and again. Reggie finally answered it.

"Don't hang up on me again," The Donation Man

said with a quiet sneer in his voice.

"I would like to speak to your supervisor, please!"

"Oh, I don't think you would. What you need to do is donate, and I won't call you again. I know you're some fancy reporter. I looked you up on the Internet, so you must have money. Ten dollars won't break your pocketbook, ma'am," he said, now back to his usual even, almost sweet voice.

Reggie felt the heat of anger rising within her. She did not like this man knowing more than her name. She was tempted to give him the ten dollars just to get him to stop calling, and maybe, just maybe, he would go away and her fear would calm. However, she could not let him bully her. "I do not wish to donate anything. Not even a dollar."

There was a long pause, then an almost purring sound in The Donation Man's voice. "Talk to you tomorrow, Reggie, and have a good day."

She heard a loud click.

Suddenly, there was a honk outside. Reggie looked out the window and saw the station's SUV. She gathered up her things, feeling very annoyed, and started to breathe deeply to calm down before seeing Jane. "Suck it up, girl," she told herself.

She made sure Lucy had food, locked the door, and jumped in the SUV with Jane.

By the time they were at Mardi Gras World,

Jane had Reggie laughing with stories of what Jane's husband had cooked for dinner and all the shenanigans her son was getting into. When they went in, they were greeted by the person in charge of events, and began a tour like the average tourist would.

Reggie and Jane were both like little girls when they learned they could dress in the Mardi Gras costumes and take pictures. Afterward, they watched a fascinating film on the history of Mardi Gras and what happens today. The guide was funny and more than willing to talk all about the history of the place. As they finished the tour they were each given a sample of King Cake, which had them raving about what a fun place this had been. There were a few retakes, and the place let them take some extra video shots for the documentary, but all-in-all, by lunchtime they were done.

It was going to be another scorcher in the city. Getting done early and having the shoot inside today was a godsend for Reggie. She was still trying to get used to the heat. As if someone was tapping into her brain, her phone rang. For just a second, she thought, *No it could not be the man again,* before answering.

"Hey, Reggie." She sighed with relief when she heard Annie's voice on the other end.

"Hey, Annie. What's up?"

"I have some bad news."

"What is it?" Reggie asked, rubbing her forehead.

"Our central air is not working. It was doing fine last night, but is not functioning now. Maybe that was the sound you heard last night. It could have been a belt or some other part grinding against something. I called the landlord, and he is sending someone over to fix it today or tomorrow. I hope it can be fixed today, but I don't know. Looks like we will be taking ten showers instead of the New Orleans two today."

"Darn! I was just going to pick up a few things and work from home since we have no interviews in the afternoon. Well, I will say New Orleans has excellent air conditioning in most of its restaurants, and the news station does, too. You could meet us down here if you want to after work."

"No, it's fine. We have air at the clinic so the animals are fine, and I think I will stay here later anyway. There are a few very sick animals I want to help since one of the staff is out sick today."

Typical Annie, Reggie thought. It did not surprise her that Annie was going to stay and help out, as she had done that before. Annie was stunning and funny, and Reggie wished she could think of someone to fix her up with.

Their landlord would let in the repair person and wait in the house until they were done. They couldn't ask for a nicer landlord, but Reggie thought of Lucy and knew she had to get her to a cooler place and make sure she had lots of water. *Guess we will be sleeping downstairs in the living room tonight if it's not fixed,* Reggie thought, getting the slightest feeling of discomfort.

"Thanks, Annie. You know, I think I might change my mind and go back home later. I worry about Lucy. Have a good day."

"You too."

Reggie ended the call.

"What's up?" Jane asked.

"Air out at home, but should be fixed by tomorrow."

"Do you want to stay at our place, Reggie? You can use the same couch as before."

"No, that's okay. I will just work most of the day from the station after we have lunch, then use the portable fan I have and sleep downstairs. Thanks anyway. If it doesn't go on tomorrow, I'll take you up on your offer." Reggie took a deep breath before continuing. "I gave Lucy lots of water, and the blinds are closed tightly anyway while I am at work."

The station did not build in emergency money for staying at hotels. She often wondered what would happen if another big hurricane came her way. What would she do? She hoped that would never happen, for everyone's sake. The station did give a food allowance, and since the Mardi Gras Museum was near her favorite broiled oyster spot, Dragos, she begged Jane to let her pick the restaurant today. Jane wasn't a big fan of oysters, but she would get her bowl of gumbo or shrimp etouffee.

After a great lunch, they headed to the station to show the footage to the boss, Stuart, and get his final approval. Only once or twice had he asked them to go back and get some more footage he felt was missing. As Reggie worked with him more, and with Jane's help, she got a better idea of what he expected.

"Great work," Stuart said as he finished the footage. "It's amazing how the people of this city pull together, no matter what."

Stuart was born and raised in New Orleans, and had the look of a New Orleans businessman. He had brown, slightly wavy hair, was about six feet tall, and wore a tan New Orleans lightweight suit that was perfect for summer. He had not left during Katrina, and was lucky to still be alive today. They wanted to transfer him to another city, but he refused, saying, "I won't leave the city." He kept his employees longer than most bosses because he was willing to work long hours like his staff, and warmth and caring oozed from him. Reggie was loyal to Sam, but if he had not come into her life, Stuart would be the kind of man she was attracted to.

"I think that we need about another month or two of shooting, and then we can actually take the time to edit this thing into an excellent documentary on the city. The tourist bureau will love it, and this really shows how the people of this city pull together, no matter what. By the end of two more months, it will be great." Stuart gave them a big smile. "How about we go to the Quarter and get a drink, ladies?"

"Sorry, Stuart," Jane said. "Time to head home to my family, and Reggie is heading back to a non-air-conditioned apartment and the love of her life."

"You mean Sam is in town?" Stuart asked, surprised.

Jane laughed. "No, I mean the real love of her life. Lucy, her cat."

"Oh, then I take it back, ladies." He laughed. "You all go and be with your gang, and since I don't have someone at home waiting for me, I will hit one of my joints for a beer and crawfish on the way home."

Reggie walked over and patted him on the shoulder. "Stuart, if I were not worried about my place and Lucy, I would love to go with you."

"And if my family was not waiting for me, you sure as hell know I would be there. Hey, maybe you can tell me I have to work, and this is a business dinner." Jane chuckled, her eyes dancing with her grin.

"No way!" he said. "Go home, now. That's an order!"

***

Jane dropped Reggie off. When she went into the house, it was not terribly hot. But the minute she walked in, Lucy came running to greet her and begged for food. No matter how much Reggie fed Lucy, she was always hungry. Lucy also always wanted to cuddle close to Reggie, regardless of where she sat.

"Okay, my pal, we're sleeping downstairs tonight, and we are both going to stay cool."

They settled into a night of Reggie working, eating dinner, talking to Sam, and more showers. Reggie's nervousness faded as she drifted off into one of the best sleeps she had had in days.

When she woke up the next morning, she was drenched in sweat. She knew to get up and hydrate herself with water and juice with potassium, and to give Lucy more water. She showered, dressed, then called Annie to see if she had heard anything more about the repairman.

"The landlord said that he was coming soon. He was able to get a rush repair, but being summer, everyone's air seems to be going out."

"Thank God!" Reggie replied. "I can be here in

the morning to let him in." As if on cue, the doorbell rang. "He just showed up," Reggie said. "Talk to you later, Annie."

The repairman looked to be in his seventies, and had the look of someone who knew exactly what he was doing. "So, let's see where the problem is. Where is your unit?"

"Out back, let me show you," replied Reggie.

As the repairman started to look at the unit and walk around her place, her phone rang.

"Reggie here," she said quickly.

"Glad you are there," came the familiar deep voice through the phone.

Reggie felt herself flush with anger, but her stomach also clenched with fear.

"Now, I said I was going to call. I knew after sleeping on it, you would donate. Since you haven't, there have been those that may have suffered because of you," he said with no anger, but some other emotion she could not distinguish.

"Enough, enough. I don't know who you are, but you have no right to keep bothering me like this," she said, bending over her desk to grab a pen. "Would you please connect me with your supervisor?"

"Of course I will, ma'am, but it will do you no good. I have a feeling you will donate whether you talk to my supervisor or not," he said in a voice that seemed to mock her.

"I would like to tell them to take me off the list and that you are not to call me again!"

"I am sorry, ma'am, but my supervisor does not like to take calls from people who have a problem with anger."

"What?" Reggie sputtered. "I don't have a problem with anger!" She was angry but tried to calm down. "Will you please let me talk to your supervisor, now?"

"No. It is evident that you are angry, and unless you calm down, I will not let you talk to them. If you get our donation package, I am sure you will be so happy with helping others that you will calm down. It may even solve your anger problem," The Donation Man said, as if he were talking to a child who had just had a temper tantrum.

Reggie felt a bit confused by his approach, but again said, "I would like to speak to your supervisor, please. I am calm, but I need to speak with them."

"Are you going to donate?"

"No, I am not. And frankly, you are the one that has convinced me not to donate."

"So, if I let you talk to my supervisor, you will donate?"

"I didn't say that, but please let me talk to your supervisor."

Suddenly The Donation Man said, "Sure, you can speak to him."

There was a click and a soft, "Can I help you?"

Reggie did not know if the person on the line was a man or a soft spoken female, but she tried to speak in a calm but firm tone to this person. "I usually donate, but I have to tell you that your representative has been too pushy. I have been called when I said I do not want to donate, and I asked that my name be taken off the list. The calls are still coming and the man who calls, I feel, is harassing me about this. Please take my name off the list!"

"We certainly will, ma'am. Let me verify your phone number and address first."

Reggie gave him her address and thought to herself. *Finally, this is all over.*

Again the soft voice said, "Thank you for calling, Ms. Page. Your name will be taken off the list, and you have also proven to us what we knew…that our employee needs to find a different job, and with all the complaints will be fired today."

Reggie didn't mean for it to go that far and hoped they would have a talk with The Donation Man, but not fire him.

"I don't know about firing him, but it sounds like someone needs to train him for phone donations, and when he is being too pushy."

"We will handle it from here, Ms. Page."

"Thank you," Reggie said.

As she started to hang up the phone, she heard, "We all have to give in life, because if we don't, it will come back to haunt us."

Reggie hung up the phone with a bad feeling, the words repeating in her head.

We all have to give in life because if we don't, it come back to haunt us. We all have to give in life because if we don't, it will come back to haunt us.

"Oh, my god. Oh, my god. Oh, my god!" Reggie said, her mouth dry and suddenly recognizing the phrase. "It was him."

CHAPTER 7

Reggie felt bile climb up her throat. She took a deep breath to keep from throwing up. She started pacing and told herself she must be wrong, but always ended up with the same thought, *Oh, my god it was him, not his supervisor, and I have pissed him off.* Then the sickening thought came to her as her hands started to sweat. *I gave him my address. Oh, my god, I gave him my address!* She ran to the kitchen sink and threw up.

Reggie pulled off a paper towel to wipe her mouth and dug into her purse to get her cell phone. She did not usually call Sam during the day, but she dialed his number as fast as she could. She was so upset that by the time Sam answered on the third ring and said, "Hi, Reggie. What's up?" she answered him in an almost breathless voice.

"Sam, I have a problem, and I need your advice.

Remember that Donation Guy I told you about yesterday?"

"Sure, the pushy one."

"Well, he got even pushier. He called again, and when I asked to talk to his supervisor, I got someone who sounded like a woman, and I told her about him. She thanked me and said she was going to fire him. But, before she hung up, she said the exact phrase he has said to me, and I think, Sam, it was him trying to disguise his voice."

"Are you sure it was him?"

"No, I can't be sure, but I think it was the same phrase he used."

"Reggie, I know this guy has scared you, and I know you are still healing from being chased and shot by The Bomber, but a lot of organizations have almost a script they use when calling people. That woman was probably just using the same line she told your Donation Man to use."

Reggie felt herself relax a little at what Sam said. It did make sense. Maybe she was blowing this all out of proportion. "I also feel like a fool for giving my address for verification to be taken off the list. I never give my address or any personal information on the phone."

"Reggie, this man is not going to come and get you. If anything, you helped some other people avoid this guy. Sorry she fired him over his calls, though. As I said before, they probably did not train the guy very well."

"You're right, Sam. I am just afraid he will be angry at me for getting him fired, and now he knows my address. I know I have PTSD from before, but something about this guy sends chills down my back!"

"Speaking of that fine back of yours," Sam said, trying to lighten the mood. "I look forward to giving you the best back rub when I see you. And maybe other areas of your gorgeous body."

Reggie laughed.

"Really Reggie, this will all blow over. This guy is probably in some state far away from you. If I thought you were in danger, I would fly right down there," Sam said.

"Okay boss, I will forget all this and focus on my new assignment in the city tomorrow."

"How about we Skype before bed, and I can tell you all about what is going on here, and mainly just stare into your eyes and throw kisses to you."

Reggie smiled, thinking how Sam was one of the most passionate men she had ever met. He was not afraid to show most of his feelings, and she did not have to drag them from him. She remembered he, too, had been shot by The Bomber, and that was something he did not want to bring up. Sam had been shot before on the job, but not as seriously as the attack from The Bomber.

"Sounds good to me. I am calling my parents to say hello, but other than that I am all yours. Sorry to interrupt you during work hours, Sam. I was just scared, and you are the one I call when I am scared."

"That's fine, and I don't mind at all. But I really have to go, Reggie. We have those shoplifters to catch, and I'm lead on the case."

"Bye, love you."

"Love you, too. Be safe, Reggie."

CHAPTER 8

Reggie settled in to give her parents a call. Their ice cream store was always busy, but the late afternoon was a good time of day to call them as they were done and home. The night manager, her cousin, would be running the small store instead. Her folks were retired, and finally had their dream job of running an ice cream parlor where they could chat with all the tourists and their friends, and still run a successful business.

Just as she started to dial their number, the doorbell rang. She couldn't help the slight twinge of nervousness she felt. She saw a man with a uniform on and the air conditioning company logo on his hat. *Thank goodness*, she thought to herself.

Reggie walked over and opened the door to a tall, smiling man who said, "You're all set. It was an easy problem to fix. I can't guarantee that it will never break again, and we are talking to your landlord about a new unit, but for now, it should do you well. Remember on real hot and sunny days to try to keep your blinds closed to keep some of the heat out, and not to turn it too low and overtax the unit."

"Thanks so much," Reggie said.

"Have a good day," he said as he headed out, his phone ringing. "On to my next stop."

Reggie was almost giddy as she picked up Lucy and started saying how lucky they were to finally get cool air. She texted Annie to tell her they were all set.

Annie texted back, *Yay!*

Reggie sat at the kitchen table and got her papers out, deciding to call her parents later. Besides, she had so much to review, and their next assignment for tomorrow was to ride along on one of the city tours. She would be covering in detail some of the tourist spots, but she wanted an overview of the city's highlights to showcase the city and fill in some of the DVD down the road.

Reggie liked the tour guides on the buses because they provided some of the personal stories about the rebuilding of the city and how their families had been affected by Katrina. They also told fun stories about life in New Orleans. Reggie got out her tour books and started her research.

After working for a few hours, Reggie decided to

call her parents. She dialed their number and heard her mom answer. Her parents did not have a caller ID, so when her mom heard Reggie's voice, she started laughing.

"I was hoping it was you! I was missing you a lot today and just needed to hear your cheerful voice. How are you?" asked her mom.

"Better now, Mom. Our air was out, but it's all fixed. I wish I had some of your ice cream just about now."

"I wish you were here too. Your dad and I are thinking of coming to see you down there, and you can be our personal tour guide if that is okay? We never get away it seems, and we both think it has been way too long since we gave you a real hug."

Reggie really missed their hugs. After she had been shot by The Bomber, her mom and dad had come to take care of her for a while, and also helped her not be so frightened by every loud sound.

"I would love that, Mom! Just let me know when you would like to come, and I can make the arrangements. Would you want to stay here or do you want a hotel downtown?"

"We would be coming to see you for three nights, so how about if we stay with you?"

"Sounds good to me. If the air goes out, I will get you a hotel downtown, and I will bring Lucy and myself there too," Reggie laughed.

They caught up on all sorts of things, and Reggie talked to her dad.

"Okay, Mom and Dad. Let me know when you want to come, and it is a done deal. Be prepared to eat the best food in the country...besides your cooking of course, Dad."

"Bye, honey. Take care and be careful. Love you."

"Love you, too," Reggie said, feeling sad they were not nearby.

When she hung up, Reggie felt a twinge of guilt for not having told her parents about The Donation Man. She knew they would just worry. Besides, he would not call again.

CHAPTER 9

As usual, Lucy's kisses awoke Reggie and her day began.

She met Jane in the French Quarter in front of a hotel to catch the city tour bus. They picked a popular tour and received permission beforehand to film a few shots of the sights, film the tour guide, and have a camera on the bus. With modern-day cameras, it was easy to not have everyone wondering what was going on. They looked like any other tourist ready to see the sights. If they did film some of the people on the bus, those people had to sign a waiver that it was okay to use their images and voices. Fortunately, with modern technology, they could do that with their phones and get a signature.

The bus was filled with a mixture of young and old, including tourists from other countries, and they had a tour guide whose loud laugh told Reggie they were in for an enjoyable morning. Most of the tours were three or four hours long with stops, so Reggie had brought lots of sunscreen for the day. They sat at the front of the bus to get better shots of the tour guide and tape some of her comments. As they went to other hotels to pick up people, Reggie filled in Jane on the house. Jane told her all about her evening as well. Reggie even handed Jane her sunscreen and laughed, saying, "Compliments of my mom!" Reggie's mom always told her not to get sunburned, to wear a hat, and to make sure to have plenty of things to drink. Reggie smiled to herself and thought no matter what age she would be, her mom would always give her tips on how to stay healthy. "I can hear my mom now, saying, 'Reggie, don't you get sunburned. And when I say have plenty of liquids, I don't mean lots of drinks in the Quarter.'"

Jane smiled and said, "Boy, you're lucky to have a mom that cares so much about you!"

"You're right, I am lucky," Reggie replied, glad to be reminded how her mom was not trying to annoy her but trying to make sure she was safe.

The tour started at the Quarter, with its history, then moved on to the other areas of the city and even out to Lake Pontchartrain and City Park, a beautiful park where they could stop for donuts and coffee. Since Reggie had her usual peanut butter on bread for breakfast, sharing a little with Lucy, she was hungry for her midmorning snack.

After their brief stop at City Park, where the guide pointed out some of the places nearby that were flooded during Hurricane Katrina, they went to one of the cemeteries. They were built above ground because of the low sea level, and they did not want bodies to float away. Some of the tombs were almost a work of art. The buildings often times housed many from the same family. Today there were lots of tour groups, and the cemetery seemed almost crowded. Reggie thought of the childish joke her dad had said once about people "dying to get in," but scolded herself for laughing a little. Death was not funny, it was sad, but something in remembering how her dad said it made her smile.

As the people followed the tour guide, Reggie decided to go back to look more closely at the inscription on one of the tombs they had just passed. It had a statue in front of it, and she was curious about what it meant. "I'll catch up with you in a few minutes," she told Jane.

As she stood before the tomb, she moved closer as one of the other tour groups was moving by her. Reggie wanted to make out what it said on the tomb. It was a family tomb, and she figured out the age of each member when they died. When she saw one that was a child, she felt her heart break at thinking one so young could die.

Suddenly she felt a shove that made her stumble and fall to the ground. "Ouch!" she said, getting back up and dusting off her scraped knee.

"Are you okay?" one of the people asked, looking concerned.

"I took a fall, but I'm annoyed at whoever bumped into me didn't stop to apologize. Thanks so much," she said to a middle-aged black woman. "Please go ahead with your group. Really, I am okay."

Reggie caught up with her tour group, and Jane, seeing her skinned knee, said, "Reggie, what happened?"

"Some rude person bumped into me and knocked me down. Didn't even bother to say they were sorry."

"Glad you're okay!"

"I am fine, just annoyed. But hey, this tour is too exciting to fret," she said, putting on a BAND-AID that her mom told her to always carry in her purse, with antibiotic cream, for occasions like this. They continued on their tour and ended up back in the Quarter just in time for lunch. There was so much history that the tour guide gave Jane extensive notes to help with the documentary. They had met a few very friendly people on the bus, and when asked if Reggie and Jane would like to join them for lunch, they said, "Sure." They had a grand time with the group, and Reggie and Jane were happy the group picked one of the restaurants they loved on Bourbon Street.

Their boss, Stuart, liked when they mixed with tourists because it gave them a perspective of what the tourists liked and how they felt about the city. Sometimes Reggie would say she was doing a documentary of the city, and if the tourists were coming to the city for the first or tenth time, what would they want to see?

Reggie and Jane were going to go back to work and started to maneuver around the crowds. It was nice to see so many tourists and New Orleans getting the visitors it deserved, but at certain times during the day, Reggie and Jane had to charge forward through the crowds to get to their work.

"Let me stop for one minute, Reggie. I promise I will be quick. I promised my son I would get him this T-shirt he thought was hilarious, and this place always has the best prices. His birthday is coming up next week," Jane said.

"Of course, go. I will be out here."

Reggie stood outside listening to the wonderful jazz coming from the various places on Bourbon Street. When the time came for her to leave this place, she knew she would miss so much about it.

Just then a wave of tourists and locals going back to work from lunch passed her by. She suddenly felt a painful pinch on her back. This time she really winced in pain. Her stomach felt sick, and her blood pressure was low, causing her to get faint with the pain. She quickly moved to a bare spot in a courtyard entrance next door.

"Reggie?" She heard Jane call out, "Where are you?"

"Over here, Jane," Reggie said.

"Are you okay?" Jane rushed over to Reggie, who was lying on the ground.

"No, I got stung or something on my back. It *really* hurts! Could you check it for me, Jane?"

Jane bent down and carefully lifted the back of Reggie's shirt. "Did you bump into anything, Reggie? It doesn't look like a bee sting, but like you hit something."

"No, but it hurts like hell. It almost feels like the time when I was little, and this kid pinched me so hard I almost passed out." Reggie saw the look on Jane's face and said, "Oh, my god, do you think someone pinched me?"

Jane said in a quiet voice, "I don't know, but with you being shoved and now this, I'm getting worried about you."

"Who would want to hurt me?"

It sounded good when she said it, but as she got up, her back started stinging. Reggie felt this sick feeling in her stomach, not from the pain, but from that part inside her saying someone was trying to hurt her. Couldn't happen twice in one year. Couldn't be hunted twice. *Oh, God,* she thought, *please don't let it be happening again.*

CHAPTER 10

When they walked into the studio, they immediately went to Stuart's office to show him some highlights of the day's taping.

"Hi ladies," said Stuart, then he grinned, genuinely glad to see Reggie and Jane standing in his door.

"Hey, Stuart," Jane said. "Can we show you some of the good stuff we filmed today?"

"Sure...." When looking at Reggie's face, he must have known something was not right. She usually came right in and said something funny, but today, she hung back and must have looked preoccupied.

Jane came in and put their tablet in front of him to look at.

"Before we start...Reggie," Stuart asked, "are you okay?"

"Not really, Stuart," Reggie answered, sitting

down in his office chair.

"So, am I going to have to drag it out of you?" Stuart's forehead lifted with worry. "What is going on?"

Jane started to answer for Reggie, but Reggie interrupted. She told Stuart the story about the cemetery and downtown.

"Probably just bad luck that I got pushed, and someone probably bumped into or pinched me with their package, or more than likely their shopping bag, when we passed. With all that has happened before I came here, it frankly has me rattled," she said.

"I'm sorry this happened, Reggie," Stuart said. "What can I do?" Stuart's left eyebrow rose as it did when he was concerned.

"I'd ask you for one of those spy cameras to wear." Reggie laughed for the first time that afternoon. "But, I think that's pushing it a little. What I would really like is for us to get back to work, so I can just forget this happened today. We had such a good time, and I'm excited to see how the taping turned out. I think we are getting excellent footage, and when this is out in three months, we'll have a winner."

"Okay, let's do this," Jane said as she began the footage.

They spent about two hours going over the footage, and were quickly able to decide what parts were the keepers and what they wouldn't use. They had many places to go and people to interview, and their deadline was coming up for the first viewing by the station staff, who wanted to come, have some po' boy sandwiches and beer, and give feedback. Besides, it had been some of the station staff, including Stuart and Jane, who'd given suggestions of who to interview and what might be interesting for the documentary. They still had to interview some of the old time New Orleans people; educators, musicians in the Quarter, students going to the local colleges, and some of the people in the various community centers in the city.

"Great work," Stuart said. "Really gives a feel of the city and makes me, even though I live here, want to visit." He laughed. "So Reggie, is your air fixed yet?"

"Thank goodness, yes!"

"Then how about I take you both to dinner tonight for all your hard work?" Stuart asked, hoping they would say yes. He could call up one of his friends, but it seemed most of them were married these days, and although he had a beautiful apartment in the garden district, he could use a night of not thinking about not having anyone to go home to.

"Sounds good to me, Stuart!" Reggie said. "How about you, Jane? Will your guys let you come out, eat dinner, and walk on Bourbon or hear jazz in the market? I left food for Lucy and my air is fixed, so I don't need to rush home."

"Sorry, you two go tonight," Jane replied, then saw the sad look on Stuart's face and Reggie's look of, *Come on, Jane, we need you!* "Sure, let me call the guys. But, I can't be out too late as frankly, I am tired, but I will go for the dinner part. Especially if work is paying!" She laughed.

"Of course, but with the three of us eating, the head boss is going to shake his head when he sees the bill." Stuart chuckled. The bond between Stuart, Reggie, and Jane was obvious to others in the office, and they too felt like a part of this hard working but fun team.

***

They wandered around the Quarter until all three could agree on a restaurant. They ate, they laughed, and Jane and Reggie even pointed out girls that might potentially be good for Stuart. By the time they had eaten and walked around a little, all three said they were tired and wanted to go home.

Stuart drove Reggie home. As they drove, they talked about her family, his parents, who had relocated to Michigan to work for the university in Ann Arbor, and all sorts of other fun things. As they got to her house, she saw Annie on the porch in her rocker, reading. Annie watched as they pulled up and waved.

Suddenly, Reggie got an idea and turned to Stuart. "I want you to meet my neighbor for a minute, Stuart."

They got out of the car and walked up to Annie. She smiled at them and got out of the chair.

"Annie, this is Stuart, my boss and friend."

"Hi," Annie replied, smiling as she shook his hand. Annie was so genuine and radiated such warmth that she just might be a good match for Stuart.

"Hi. I see you have the perfect place to read. A rocker and a book...paradise," Stuart said to Annie.

"I do love to read out here, but with my schedule, I don't get as much time as I would like."

"What do you do?" Stuart asked.

As Reggie saw the two of them were hitting it off, she yawned and said. "Okay, you guys, I am exhausted. Why don't you two continue your conversation, and I'm going in to relax and to feed Lucy. Thanks for the ride, Stuart. I'll see you tomorrow."

They both smiled at Reggie's suggestion, and Annie cleared off the other rocker for Stuart as Reggie went into the house.

Lucy ran to Reggie as she walked in, and rubbed

against her leg with affection. It was also her way to tell Reggie she was starving.

"Okay, Lucy, I'll feed you."

Reggie walked into the kitchen, then realizing her side still hurt, told Lucy, "I'm going to need to change into my comfortable robe and nightgown so I can settle in for the evening, too."

Just as she started to climb the steps, the phone rang. She reached into her pocket to answer it.

"Hello, Reggie here," she said, hoping it was Sam.

There was no one on the line, and she did not recognize the number.

"Hello...hello? Is anyone there?"

Silence. Dead silence.

Reggie hung up the phone, but it rang again.

"Hello, who is this?"

There was still silence on the line, but Reggie was sure she heard breathing.

"Hello, this is not funny. Maybe the phone is broken, and you can't hear me?"

Nothing.

Then suddenly the phone went dead.

She felt nervous, and once upstairs, called Sam to see if he had called from a work phone or line.

Sam's calm voice got somber as he said, "I don't like this, Reggie. I want to come down for a few days and be with you."

"No, absolutely not, Sam! I am a little nervous, but I am sure I am overreacting. Come see me in two weeks like we planned."

"Are you sure? I love you and worry about you, Reggie. You know that."

"And I love you too, Sam, but I can't have you running here trying to protect me when I am scared. Besides, today was just obnoxious tourists, and the phone call was probably a mistake," Reggie said, trying to convince herself. Reggie and Sam talked longer, and Reggie told Sam the things she wanted to do to his body when they next were together.

"This is an X-rated phone call, Reggie!"

"I don't do sexting or anything like that, but I do like to tell you on the phone how much I want to kiss you and hold your body against me."

"Tell me more, tell me more," Sam begged as Reggie settled in to tell him more.

CHAPTER 11

"So what did you think of Stuart?" Reggie asked Annie as they both left for work.

Annie smiled. "Actually, Reggie, I liked him. We stayed on the porch for a while...he's very comfortable to chat with. I did not feel he put on any airs or was trying to over-impress me. He seems to be just a nice guy."

"So is that good?" Reggie asked.

"Yes, that is great. I am at the age now where I am not looking for the world's handsomest guy, but someone attractive and just a real person who would be kind, and of course funny."

"Sooo, are you going to see him again?" Reggie asked.

"As a matter of fact, Ms. Matchmaker, we are going to meet in the Quarter and have dinner there one night this week," Annie said with an amused look in her eyes.

"Yay!" Reggie shouted. "He really is nice, and he got so shafted by his last girlfriend —"

"Don't tell me too much, Reggie! Some things are better left unsaid at this point."

"Okay, okay. I'll head to work. Jane and I have another shoot, and today we're going outside of the city on one of the bayou tours. Wish me luck that we don't get eaten by an alligator," Reggie said, pretending she had an alligator hanging from her leg. Reggie loved that she could be silly with Annie. "Any animal crisis today at the clinic?"

"Nope, we just have a lot of sick animals with this heat. And if I see one more poor animal that has been left in a hot car or left on a chain outside in this heat, I am going to scream! I wish people would not own animals and think they are just things they don't have to pay attention to."

"Me too. But you know I'm crazy about Lucy."

Annie got into her car and said, as she was about to leave, "It's too bad you don't have more animals. You are the perfect parent for them. Really, I mean it, Reggie. If you're ever a mom, you will be great. And can you imagine what gorgeous babies you and Sam would have?"

"Don't even go there, Annie," Reggie said, actually frowning. She loved Sam, but it sounded so serious when Annie talked of children, even jokingly. "Have a good day, Annie." Reggie waved as she walked to the street car.

Her phone rang, and thinking, *Thank goodness it's ringing now before I get out in the boonies*, she answered. She did not recognize the number, so she used her formal voice, "Hello, this is Reggie."

No answer.

"This is Reggie. I can't hear you. Can you hear me?"

No answer.

Just as she was ready to hang up, she heard a voice say, "You're a bad person, and I hope you rot in hell."

"What did you say?" Reggie asked, clenching the phone closer to her ear, sure she'd heard wrong.

This time the person on the other end spoke louder. "I said you're a bad person, and I hope you rot in hell!"

Reggie's legs started to buckle as she recognized the soft voice. "Leave me alone, whoever you are." Reggie wanted to scream, feeling her whole body start to shake and bracing her body against one of the poles so she did not lose her balance.

"You're a bad person, and I hope you rot in hell. In fact, I am here to make sure that happens!"

"You're...here?" Reggie whispered in disbelief.

"Here. There. And now, I will be everywhere. Sorry you got hurt yesterday. Guess those tourists can be a rowdy bunch," he said with a leering undertone.

"OH...MY...GOD," Reggie breathed. "You're here in New Orleans?"

Silence was all that met Reggie's ears.

CHAPTER 12

Reggie felt sick to her stomach, and kept looking in all directions hoping The Donation Man was not following her. She jumped on the trolley and headed to the office to meet Jane before going to see the alligators.

She kept looking around her, but didn't see anyone on the street outside the office, so she went upstairs and saw Jane leaning over papers at her desk.

Jane glanced up at her face. "Reggie, you're as pale as a ghost. Are you ill?"

Reggie felt clammy, and her heart was pounding. "No, it is that damn Donation Man. He called me again, Jane, and said he was in town. Remember when I got pushed? Well, he must have done it, because he mentioned it on the phone. Oh my god, this is nuts!"

"You look scared, Reggie. Let's head out, and I want you to tell me more. Don't worry, I have your back." Jane put an arm around Reggie's shoulders, and they headed out to Jane's car.

Jane drove out to the bayou tour. Tension filled the air in the car, and Reggie shook the whole way there while telling Jane about the phone call.

"I would love to tell you that you have nothing to worry about, but you know I would be lying, Reggie. This nut has it in for you, and as harmless as I thought he was before, you were pushed yesterday. In fact, twice."

"You're right, Jane. He is pissed at me, and I think he meant it when he said I should rot in hell."

Reggie started playing with her hair as they drove, something she hadn't done for a long time. After almost getting killed by The Bomber, she had pulled so much of her hair out from stress that she thought she might have to get a wig. A tough lady she was, but who would have thought she of all people, newsperson or not, would get two really crazy people trying to hurt her in two years?

"Reggie," Jane said, lightly patting her hand. "I think it's time to involve the law. Why don't you go tell someone in the police department about this after our tour? And for God's sake, call Sam. Tell him what's going on."

Reggie hung her head, realizing she did not even know what this guy looked like. She thought he was a guy, but who knew? He could be right beside her, and she wouldn't know it was him…except there was something about his voice.

When they arrived at the docks, Reggie decided she would call Sam later. But for now, she wanted to go on the tour and forget The Donation Man had even called.

The boat was not full for some reason, which was unusual from what Reggie had heard, because taking a tour of the swamps was a fun time for tourists. Reggie had never done this before, so she was curious to see why everyone loved the tours, and they could get good shots for the documentary.

Jane told Reggie she had gone on a tour and loved it, but she was not one for snakes and alligators, so she was not going to do too many shots where she had to stand close to live reptiles. Reggie had always been sort of a tomboy growing up. She loved to play baseball, look at toads, get muddy, and she loved looking at the reptile exhibits in the zoos. She'd heard she could get a picture of her holding a baby alligator, and she was so excited.

As she was getting her ticket for the boat her excitement soared. And then she thought of the phone call earlier and almost felt nauseous.

"Why don't you give Sam a quick call, Reggie?" Jane suggested with a concerned look growing on her face.

"I guess I could call him for a few minutes and fill him in."

Reggie got her phone out and tried to reach Sam. The connection wasn't good, but she left a message on his voice mail. She didn't give him all the details, and tried to keep her voice calm.

CHAPTER 13

As they walked back to the SUV, laughing at the good time they had on the tour, and how Jane still kept her distance from the alligators, they noticed a piece of paper on the windshield. "Oh no, even flyers out here." Jane laughed, grabbed it, and read it. She frowned and scrunched it up into a ball.

"What did it say?" Reggie asked.

"I'm taking you to the police station now!" Jane said, her eyes shining with fury. "It said, 'Found You.'"

"Oh shit!" Reggie said, smoothing her hair. "I agree. I want to tell them what's going on. They may think I am wacky, but now I'm actually getting scared."

They spent the afternoon at the police station talking to a Sergeant Raymond, a big burly guy who had a way of listening to Reggie that made her tell him everything and even relax some. Reggie did mention her boyfriend was a policeman, but was in another city. She knew to give the sergeant the crumpled piece of paper she had retrieved in case there were any fingerprints on it.

"I believe you, but are you sure this isn't some fan playing a prank on you, or one of your friends with a weird sense of humor?"

She hesitated on whether to tell him about almost being killed last year by The Bomber, but she did. She could tell he seemed a little skeptical after she told him the story. Reggie told him to go on the Internet, and he would see it was real. Because she was not a local news reporter and doing a documentary, she certainly was not a celebrity to the sergeant. With Jane being a local the sergeant seemed to aim his questions at her the most.

He logged it all on the computer and said he would call Reggie if they found out anything.

Reggie and Jane knew they had to do their check in with Stuart about the tour, and Reggie knew she would have to tell him all about The Donation Man.

Stuart was sitting at his desk with his shoulders hunched over, eyeing a rough draft of a story. He heard them walk in the door, looked up, and smiled. "Hello, ladies, so where is my alligator?" He laughed.

Reggie glanced at Jane, and they both started

laughing as they pulled out a stuffed toy alligator and put it on his desk, all the while making alligator sounds. Reggie loved to laugh at their pranks, so tears were streaming down her face when she heard Stuart start to snort with his belly laugh.

"Okay, mission accomplished. How was the tour?" he said as he sat back in his chair, arms behind his head with his usual "I'm ready to really listen" look.

"The tour was fabulous," Jane replied. "We got great shots along the way, and some of the stories the old timers told us about the swamps had me wishing the tour was longer."

"Yes, it was great, and we are going to leave you lots of footage if you want to go through it," commented Reggie.

"Usually I would, ladies, but since Reggie was so kind to introduce me to her neighbor, I just made late afternoon plans with her."

"You took off work?" Jane laughed. "This girl must have made a good impression on you!"

"Actually," Stuart said with a shy smile, "she is a delight. I can't believe she would want to see me again, but I think she actually wants to. Have you spoken with her, Reggie?"

"Yes, I have, Stuart, and she likes you. I know you both, and she wouldn't go out with you if she did not want to," Reggie said. She liked them both, and thought it would be nice if it worked out for them. "Now, Stuart...." Reggie hesitated before telling him more. "Something did happen today that you should know as my boss. I had to go to the police station."

"Wh...what?! Why?" Stuart sputtered as he stared at Reggie and Jane.

"I got a call from The Donation Man I told you about, and he is in New Orleans. It seems he is the one responsible for me getting pushed yesterday. He even left a note on the car that we parked at the swamp tour. For all I know, he could have been on the tour. I went to the police to report it, but there is really nothing they can do for now."

"Why don't you go stay with Jane, Reggie? If this nut knows where you live, he might try to scare you again."

"I thought of that, but I need to be in my home. I have my cat, my baseball bat, and I am going to be very careful. I promise you."

"Okay," Stuart said, not convinced Reggie was safe. "But, how about if you check in with one of us each night, and I will stop by when I drop off Annie tonight."

"Sounds good. Now, let's talk about what our next assignment is. I need to get my mind off this. Then take home some fried chicken to drown my fears." Reggie laughed half heartily.

They spent the rest of the afternoon talking about taping one of the plantations, then they headed out of the office together. Both Jane and Stuart offered to give Reggie a ride.

"I am going to take you home, Reggie," Stuart insisted. "Besides, I want to check out your place before you go in."

"Okay, boss," Reggie said, actually relieved she did not have to walk into her house alone today. Tomorrow she would be all right, but she was shaken about The Donation Man.

CHAPTER 14

The house lights were on at Annie's. Reggie had also left a light on inside her place for her cat in case she got home after dark. Stuart walked her up to the door, and they both looked inside the place to make sure no one was there. Reggie felt a little foolish, but for some reason, she felt safer after they checked.

"I am headed over to Annie's for our indoor picnic, Reggie. If you need anything, you let me know."

"Ha, you love your food. I happen to know Annie does too, so you guys are all set. Have fun. I will be fine," Reggie said, giving Stuart a quick hug and then shutting the door after he left. If she could have had a brother, she would have wanted him to be like Stuart, kind and tenderhearted.

Reggie settled in for the night with her cat, and got her stack of magazines to keep her company. She thought of giving her parents a call, but she knew they would pick up on her being upset and she did not feel like telling them. She tried to call Sam, but his phone went to voicemail.

No rain was predicted, but a beat of pouring rain pelted the house. *Oh, damn,* Reggie thought. *Please don't let me lose power. Not tonight.* Reggie got out her battery candles and flashlights just in case.

The pelting rain turned into a loud clap of thunder. "Oh shit. No," she whispered to herself as she petted her cat, trying to calm her down, as well as herself.

Suddenly the lights flickered and went out.

Reggie turned on the candles and reminded herself not to open the refrigerator in case the power would be out for a while. She got up and grabbed a bag of chips, turned on her radio, and continued to pet her cat between mouthfuls.

She almost started to doze off sitting up when she heard the banging on her door.

Must be Stuart and Annie, she thought as she headed to answer it. But it did not look like Annie or Stuart...all she could see was the shape of a tall, muscular man. The door knob started to turn as she heard someone calling her name.

"Reggie! Reggie!" they yelled over the thunder. "Open up! It's me!" Reggie started to back away from the door when she heard her lock opening up. She turned and began to run, until she heard the voice behind her yell, "Stop, Reggie! It's me, Sam!"

She spun around, her mouth dropping open, and ran to Sam, wrapping her arms around him.

"Oh, Sam. You have no idea how you scared me!"

"If your racing heart and the look on your face is any indication, I think I do. I am so sorry, Reggie. I really wasn't trying to scare you."

"What are you doing here? I thought you weren't supposed to come for a while."

"Jane called me and told me what was going on. I know I said this guy was probably harmless, but I was wrong. He sounds like someone who could really hurt you, and it sounds like he is really having mental issues with you being his target. I thought if I came down here I might be able to help the police catch this guy."

"But how can you be here? You said you have a lot of cases back home."

"I do, but I have been with the force for so long that Mike said I could come down here and take leave time. The New Orleans police are a good group of guys, so if I am lucky, they might let me work on the case. My primary concern is you, Reggie," he said, tilting her chin up gently to look into her eyes. "As you know, you are the woman of my dreams, and I don't want anything to happen to you. I love you, and we will find this guy." Sam's eyes softened as he hugged Reggie. She could feel his warmth. "In the meantime, let's make sure all your doors and windows are secure. I wish you had an alarm on your door, and maybe the landlord can help with that. Besides, I want to ravish your body." Sam's eyes crinkled with amusement. "This is a working vacation, and I will be your protector and investigator."

"Sam, last year I would have scolded you for trying to be my protector, but not this time. I am strong and independent, but I will take all the protecting I can get," Reggie whispered as she ran her fingers through his hair.

"Let's settle in for the night after we check the locks."

"Sounds good to me. Let me call Stuart and tell him you're here, so he doesn't panic if he hears noises other than my cat in the house."

They ate chips and cheese, laughed, and made passionate love. There was something about the thought of being hurt and never seeing Sam again that made his touch even more sensuous. When they kissed, it was like she was taking in every part of him. His caress, his kiss, his arms wrapped around her, all ended with an intensity that left them both breathless. As they lay in each other's arms, Sam kissed her gently and said, "I won't let anything happen to you, Reggie. We survived The Bomber, and we will survive this, too."

As they drifted asleep, Reggie heard the faintest sound of branches hitting the roof.

CHAPTER 15

Reggie's alarm went off early the next morning with its usual obnoxious sound. It was annoying on purpose, so she wanted to turn it off. It took her a few minutes to realize Sam was lying beside her. She had work, and he said he was going to go down to the police department to see if he could get any more information from the policeman Reggie spoke with yesterday. Ideally, he wanted to see the footage of the Quarter where Reggie was pushed and the cemetery, but he did not know if they would give him that.

"Hi, beautiful; ready to start the day? If we had more time, I would stay in bed with you all morning," he said, staring at her with a devilish grin on his face. "But we both have work to do."

Reggie got up, but not before kissing Sam passionately and gently smoothing his hair at the same time. She did feel more relaxed with Sam there, and felt that all was going to be okay.

"Jane and I are going to go uptown today to visit one of the shopping areas there. We have to put in something about all the fun stores that stock some interesting trendy clothes. Actually, I may keep my eye out for something for our New Orleans work party they will be having in a few weeks...I invited you. You know I don't like to spend a lot of money on clothes, but I want to wow you with something for the dance." Reggie turned and grinned as she did her model walk down the stairs to get her coffee.

Reggie heard the sound of the horn as she was pouring her coffee. "Damn, I thought I told Jane.... But I must have told her earlier," she shouted so Sam could hear.

She went out to the driveway and leaned in as Jane rolled down her window. "Come on in, Jane, and see who surprised me yesterday, as if you had nothing to do with this."

"Really? Thanks."

"I do appreciate you letting Sam know about The Donation Man. He's going to stay here and help me find this guy, or if he does more to get revenge, at least Sam will be here." Reggie gave Jane a warm smile. "I did goof up the time, so please come in and have a cup of coffee while I get dressed. You and Sam can catch up, but I promise I will be quick."

"Sounds good to me. In fact, how about if I park on your street and we walk down Carrolton Avenue towards the river, and look in those shops and film there? We really need to do Tulane University and Loyola, which are near Audubon Park, but also, it would be fun to do the shops near the campus."

"Be warned, I will be looking for a dress for the office party. You've said so much about it and how fun it is that I'm really excited about it."

Reggie realized she was not as anxious as she had been, and even heard the lightness in her voice again, not the fear.

Reggie got dressed, and Jane had a cup of coffee with Sam. Reggie couldn't help notice when she came downstairs there was a sudden silence, and a glance between Sam and Jane.

"Okay, you guys. I am here, and I know you were talking about me. But I know that between the man I love and my good friend, it was all good," she said as she blew them both a kiss. Then Reggie walked over to Sam and gave him a big kiss. "I will see you back here at around five. Good luck with the police station, and call me if anything comes up and you need to get ahold of me."

Reggie and Jane headed down the street looking for little shops they might film in. They always carried their smartphones so the owners could electronically sign the waivers, and Jane had her newest, lightest camera to film.

***

"So how are your guys, Jane? You've spent so much time hearing about my situation, I've not asked you about them."

Jane laughed and shook her head. "You know my guys, goofy as hell, but funny as can be. Nothing too new to report, except my son really likes his classes." Jane looked into the window of one of the shops. "Hey, how about you and Sam come over to our house for dinner? Jeff can whip up one of his special New Orleans dishes for you guys. I promise we won't keep you love birds too long, so you can get back to using the time you have together for some romance."

Reggie loved to eat at their house, not just because of the great food, but because of the fun and warmth there. Jane's husband and Sam had met once and hit it off.

Jane continued. "Or the next night if that is better. Let me ask Jeff, as I just found out his sugar is getting a little high, so he is cooking with a little less sugar and pasta than he used to. But don't worry, he still loves his butter when he cooks."

"Sounds good to me. Either night works."

"Let me talk to my family and see what everybody's plans are, then I'll let you know," Jane said as they walked into the first of many stores they would visit that day, including stopping at a restaurant that was a landmark for the University Area.

CHAPTER 16

Reggie and Jane got some great footage of the stores, and Reggie found a beautiful robin's egg blue tea length dress, with a subtle plunging yet tasteful neckline, that Jane said was just made for her. When Reggie asked Jane if she wanted to try on any outfits, she laughed and said, "Heavens no. I am a Levi's and black slacks with a top kind of girl. You can be the glamour girl on our team, Reggie."

Reggie realized one of the things that made her feel comfortable with Jane was how she was so down to earth, like her friend Maggie back home. Plus, Jane was comfortable with who she was. She always had to wear her lipstick and was a stunning woman, but she did not go for the so-called fashionable outfits. Reggie was curious to see what Jane would wear to the party. When she asked Jane, she laughed again and said, "You will be surprised like everyone else."

Actually, Reggie was a jeans type of girl, but she sure enjoyed dressing up at times. She liked her men in jeans, but she had never seen Sam dressed up for a formal event, and knew he would look gorgeous.

"Hey, let's go to Camellia Grill for lunch then head down to show Stuart our footage. We can edit some of it today…if you can tear yourself away from Sam, that is," Jane said, giving Reggie a grin.

"Sounds good. I need to give Lucy a little more food before we go to The Quarter, though."

They walked back to Reggie's house and Jane waited in her car.

As Reggie walked into the house, she expected to be greeted by Lucy. Reggie looked towards the kitchen, but her cat did not come running. *She must be sleeping*, she thought, and headed into the kitchen. *Damn, I left a window open*, she thought, walking over to close it.

"Lucy!" she called. "Lucy!"

Nothing.

Reggie felt her heart start to race as she began going from room to room, calling Lucy's name louder and louder.

Still nothing.

Now almost frantic, Reggie went down the hall to the last bedroom upstairs. Suddenly, there was a bumping sound from behind the closed door. *Funny,*

I don't remember leaving the door closed this morning. She opened the door, and Lucy dashed past her and down the stairs towards her food bowl.

What the hell, she thought to herself, seeing nothing in the room. Maybe Sam had shut the door, and Lucy was under the bed and he didn't know it.

She went downstairs and found Lucy under the couch, hiding. Reggie gently got her out by bribing Lucy with food. "It's okay, girl. Your mom has come home and saved your butt. I'll have to tell Sam to check before he leaves the place and make sure you're accounted for. Are you scared after being locked in a room? I bet."

She signaled to Jane that she would be out and left more food for Lucy. Making sure the windows were closed, she looked out the back window and saw a slight shadow move across the lawn. "I'm just being jittery," she whispered.

Locking the door behind her she jumped into Jane's car, and they spent the rest of the day on their project. She did take the time to call her folks and tell them about her work and Sam. She avoided getting them scared about The Donation Man incident. Funny how she tried to protect her parents like they tried to protect her by avoiding certain topics.

CHAPTER 17

Stuart hummed as they walked into his office to show him the footage. When he looked up, he said, "Thanks, ladies. I really had a good time with Annie last night. And, she wants to go out again. This time we may go to the Maple Leaf and listen to some jazz. She is terrific!"

Both Jane and Reggie were happy for Stuart, and they all quickly got through the footage and changes, with a few reshoots that needed to be done in the next couple of months before the final would be ready for editing.

"Hey, Stuart, Reggie and Sam will be coming over to our home for dinner tomorrow. Do you want to join us? Annie can come too if it's not pushing things too fast."

"I appreciate the offer, but let me take a rain check. Tomorrow Annie and I are going out, and we still are getting to know each other." A sly smile crept across Stuart's face.

"I am headed home to hear what Sam has found out, Stuart. I'll take the trolley home, as it's daytime. So no lectures," interrupted Reggie.

Stuart said, "Okay, okay, I know I am overprotective with you, but call Sam and let him know you're on the way. Sounds like The Donation Man is probably long gone, but just to be safe, it is good to have someone there for you."

"Bye. See you guys," Reggie replied as she walked out of the office.

Reggie was happy to see Sam's car in the driveway, and even happier when she walked in to smell the aroma of his cooking filling the house. Using some of the seafood that was easy to get in New Orleans, it smelled like he was making his gramma's seafood pasta.

Reggie rushed into the kitchen, and when he turned to smile, she ran up and gave him a big kiss.

"Wow, what was that for?"

"Just because I adore you and you came to help me."

"Yeah, right. You're after me for my cooking. I know you." He grinned.

"That too," Reggie said. "I am going to run upstairs and take a quick shower. Do you mind? I promise I will help you when I come down. The day is so New Orleans hot."

"Sure, gives me more time to impress my lady," he said, grinning as he gave her his sexy man pose.

Reggie turned on the shower and felt the water rush all over her body as she remembered she needed to tell Sam about closing the window and keeping the door open, so Lucy did not get locked in. She changed into a light shift and headed downstairs after taking a brief look at herself in the mirror.

"I'll set the table, and how about a New Orleans beer? That factory is on one of our films, and it was so fun that they let us sample some of the product."

"Sounds good to me," Sam said, putting her plate of spaghetti on the table and pulling out her chair. No matter how much they were together, Sam always was a true gentleman.

"Oh, Sam, do you know how lucky I am to have you, and how my parents like you?"

"That's sweet, Reggie. What do you think?" Sam motioned to his spaghetti.

"This spaghetti is excellent. I won't ask you for the recipe as I am hoping you will make it again. I am SO happy you're the one that loves to cook in this relationship! So tell me what happened today?"

"I went to the station to discuss your case, and asked them if I could get the footage for the areas you were in to see if we can find who pushed you. They were okay with that, and with me looking into the case. But I have to tell you, I got the feeling they thought this would all go away and you were probably safe now. They are giving me one of their people in technology to help with the case, who of course is working on twenty million others, I am sure. If it is like my department, there are so many good cops and so many cases, they have to prioritize. I did see there have been no other cases or complaints they know of with someone doing this."

"Oh, great," Reggie said. "I have to be the one to get this wacko on my case. I have to say no I don't want to donate and piss the guy off."

"Hey, you did nothing wrong. Sometimes it takes one person to trigger something in someone who has some mental issues. He may just love that you are scared, and that is all he needs. Has he called again?"

"No, he hasn't called. Hey, can we forget about him now and just enjoy dinner? I would love to tell you more about our shoot...and by the way, we're going to Jane's house tomorrow for dinner."

They finished dinner, had a second beer, and after watching some television, headed up to bed with Sam kissing the back of Reggie's neck the entire way upstairs.

Reggie giggled, and as she started stripping off

her dress, said, "See who can get naked the fastest!"

They both tore off their clothes and jumped into bed, pulling up the covers as they laughed and began kissing each other. Their kissing grew more intense and they quickly made love, wanting to drench their flames of desire.

As they lie, breathing hard and exhausted, holding each other, they felt the pounce of Lucy on the bed. Reggie felt Lucy's head brush against her cheek to kiss her as she did every night and morning. All of a sudden, Reggie remembered she wanted to tell Sam about the cat and the window.

Not a wonderful time for a conversation, but she turned to Sam in the glow of the room's soft light and said, "Honey, in the morning, please leave the door open for Lucy. She was locked in this morning. And please shut all the windows. The bathroom window was open, and you know I'm a little jumpy these days."

Sam sat up in bed and said, "Reggie, I never leave windows open, and you have told me many times before not to shut the door or the cat would get caught in a room. You must have been rushing to leave with Jane and forgot to close the window."

Reggie felt uneasy. She didn't remember doing those things, and he may be right, but there was a sudden feeling of lightheadedness as she thought,

Oh my god! What if it was him, The Donation Man?

Chapter 18

The next morning Reggie woke up with a headache. She'd thought about The Donation Man throughout the night, and just when she was asleep for a while, she startled awake after a vivid dream of a dark shadow grabbing her arm and not letting go.

Reggie turned over to Sam, and he smiled then frowned. "You look like hell. Are you okay?"

"Gee, thanks, that is a great way for my boyfriend to say hello in the morning!"

Sam turned red and softly said, "No, I meant to say you look like you didn't sleep last night, and are you okay?"

She gently touched his face and said, "I am fine. No, I didn't sleep much, and I had bad dreams about The Donation Man. These are times I wish I had a camera system in my house so I would feel safer, and if anyone tried anything, it would be on tape."

"What do you mean try anything?"

Reggie sighed as she said, "I didn't tell you, but I am almost positive I did not lock the cat in the room or leave the window open. I'm so worried that The Donation Man can get me that it kept me awake. I also am afraid he could hurt you, Sam."

"Reggie, let's hope that this guy made his point and is long gone. Other than me continuing to work with the police, you need to go about your business, but not alone. I'm glad we're going to Jane's tonight."

"Me too. And today, Jane and I.... Whoops, I don't want to be late like yesterday," she said, jumping out of bed after giving Sam a quick kiss. Before she left, she said, "Let yourself out and I will call you later." She couldn't stop herself from reminding him to make sure everything was locked up, and the cat was okay.

She wanted to take a morning walk, but something told her to forget it this time and just meet Jane. She looked around as she walked to the trolley car stop on Carrolton and Green Avenue, and saw there were about four people waiting there. No mad killers today, she thought as she looked at the people. Just three average looking men and one tough looking woman. Besides, The Donation Man would not be so brazen to be at her trolley stop in broad daylight. Yet she wondered, if he was at the alligator tour area, what else could he do?

"Okay, you're a reporter," she said to herself. "Note what all the people look like, and from now on, be even more aware of your surroundings and memorize everyone's face."

Reggie got on the trolley car and settled into the hardwood seats near the window, noticing all the people in the car as the trolley started to pull out. Not knowing what made her turn around in her seat, Reggie looked outside to where she'd gotten on, and noticed a man standing very still, just staring at the trolley car. Feeling a slight shiver go through her, she could see his smile under his hat that covered the rest of his face. A twisted, unnatural smile. He waved at her, and turned and walked down the next street from her house.

Quickly getting her cell phone out of her purse. Reggie's hands shook as she called Sam.

"Sam, I think The Donation Man is around. I saw this man at one of the stops, and he waved. He turned and walked down the street near my house. Be careful, Sam. Maybe he knows you are there. Oh, God, please be careful!"

"Calm down. It's okay," Sam said. "Do not come back here. It probably was just someone waving hello like they do down here. Go to work, and I promise I will be on the lookout for anyone. And remember, I have martial arts training and a gun. Remember you are trained in martial arts, too, Reggie. But let's hope you never have to use it. What did this guy look like?"

"About five feet nine inches, white, thin, and he had a hat on. But he had thick lips when he smiled. Oh, yes, he did have jeans on, and a colored T-shirt."

"Good. Again, it was probably just someone flirting with you and not your guy. But it's always good to be on the lookout. Now take a few breaths and relax. Call me when you get to work. I am going to go to the police station, but I'll stay here awhile to assure you are okay."

The woman sitting next to Reggie had heard some of the things she said, and said in a kind voice, patting Reggie's hand lightly, "Don't worry, ma'am. It will all be okay."

"I hope so," Reggie replied, still tense. "I really hope so."

CHAPTER 19

Reggie spent the day editing with Jane and Stuart. She looked forward to Sam coming to her office to tell her what he had found out from the tapes, and also to relaxing at Jane's house for dinner. Reggie had stopped by a local bakery and picked up a dessert to take over, and a six pack of beer, and some soda. Most of their friends were wine drinkers, but Jane and her husband liked beer like Reggie and Sam.

Reggie worked hard to forget about the morning. It seemed like she was doing a lot of that lately. Later in the day, as Jane and Reggie were going over the prior day's taping, Sam walked in. He waved and said, "Hello ladies," but his tone was serious.

"What's up?" Jane and Reggie said at the same time.

"You may be right, Reggie. When I went over some of the tapes today, I thought there was no way we could figure who might have pushed you, but when I went over a few seconds at a time, I noticed a guy that was in both places you were hurt. Like you said, white guy, five-nine, thin, and noticeably thicker lips."

Reggie gasped at this and put her hand to her mouth, "Oh, my god. Then it was probably him at the trolley stop!"

"Yes, and I have printed out a picture, although it's grainy and he fits the description of so many people around town. He hasn't approached you anymore, and we can't prove he pushed you, so we won't have much of a case. I told some of the guys at the station what was going on, and asked them if they had ever seen this guy before. None of them had, and when they scanned his face into their facial recognition system, nothing came up."

"Let's all go to my house and forget this creep for the evening. My husband's gumbo and a beer should take your mind off him. I am glad you're here, Sam, while this is going on!"

"Me, too," Sam said as he put his arm gently around Reggie's shoulder. "Gumbo and beer it is."

That evening Reggie was able to just laugh and eat. Sam seemed somewhat relaxed, but Reggie knew him well enough to know he was upset. Jane's dog, Lilly, kept coming up to her and licking her hand, hoping Reggie had a little gumbo on it for her to sample. When she didn't find much on Reggie's hand, she would go to Sam or Jane's son and try their hand.

"I am sorry Stuart and Annie didn't come, but they wanted time to themselves," said Jane.

"They really are a good match. Both nice and very responsible. And I know if Annie gets involved with him, she won't dump him," replied Reggie.

They all began to fade and realized it was time to end the party. Sam and Reggie helped clean up then headed to Reggie's.

On the way, Reggie and Sam started talking about if they had another pet what kind would they want. It seemed so odd, yet not odd, to be talking as if they would be together forever and what kind of pet they wanted. The glitch was where they would live. They had time to figure that out, Reggie hoped as she felt her stomach tense up.

The porch light was on when they got back to Green Street, and all looked to be in order. Reggie noticed Stuart's car was on the street and the television light through the window.

Holding hands up the walkway, Reggie got her key out to open the door. As she put it in the door, it slid open without her turning the key. "What the heck?!" she said, pushing the door open. She froze, seeing the cushions from the couch lying on the floor, books ripped apart, and something red all over the wood floor.

Sam pushed his way in front of her and said, "Go on the porch. Now!" He moved backward through the door to the front porch and called the police. Reggie stood perfectly still. She didn't know what to think, and she barely heard Sam's conversation with police over the phone. Then suddenly she realized her cat was inside still. "Oh, Lucy! I must find her," she said, running back into the house before Sam could stop her.

She ran around the house feeling as if she was crazy, but she had to find Lucy. Reggie screamed her name, "LUCY!" Upstairs and all around the bedroom, furniture was ripped, and the same red was all over the floor. Then she heard a faint sound coming from the closet.

"Don't open the door! Let me do it," Sam said, his gun aimed at the door.

He swung the door open slowly and out ran Lucy. Reggie scooped her into her arms, snuggled her close, and just stared at the damage.

Sam reached into the closet and pulled out a white piece of paper. He unfolded it and read aloud, "This did not have to happen to you, selfish bitch. I didn't kill your cat because I am the nice one. I help raise money, and you're the bitch that can't spare a dime. Guess you will have to spend money to get new furniture. You will pay for this, and not just with money. Soon…oh yes, soon."

Just as Sam finished reading the note, the phone rang. Reggie answered it and heard the familiar voice of The Donation Man. He laughed and said, "Tell your boyfriend hello from me, and he can't protect you." Then there was silence.

They suddenly heard a pounding on the door and went downstairs to find Stuart and Annie. "What the hell is going on?" asked Stuart.

"Don't come in," Sam said sternly. "That crazy person got in, and I don't want anyone else in here till after the team comes over to lift prints and analyze this place."

"Is she okay?" Stuart asked just as Reggie walked around the corner holding Lucy close to her.

"Did you guys hear anything?" Reggie asked, still in shock and disbelief.

"Nothing. In fact, we were watching a movie, and I thought I heard Lucy meow a few times but wasn't sure. Maybe some walking noises, but I thought you guys were home."

"These are times I wish I had a security camera," Reggie said. "Maybe we can look at the cams at gas stations or grocery stores closest to the house and get a better look at our guy."

"Cameras or not, Reggie, and even with me here, we are going to beef up security. I am sleeping downstairs from now on. If he even tries to come back, he will deal with me," Sam said.

"Sam, this guy is obviously unbalanced, and I don't want you hurt," Reggie said, touching his arm gently. Reggie turned pale, then turned to Annie and Stuart. "Oh, my god! You guys are in danger too. If this guy wants to punish me, he might try to hurt you, Annie."

Stuart gave Annie a concerned look. "I know this sound nuts, Annie, but maybe it is better if you came to my place until we find out more."

"Only if Sam is with Reggie twenty-four hours a day. I do not want this guy coming around her. If I had family in town, I would go there, but Stuart, I will take you up on your offer."

"Good," Reggie said. "Sam will be here, but I am not going to let this bastard hurt any of us. He thinks that I am a helpless female, but he is going to know he is messing with the wrong lady." Reggie clenched her hands into fists. "Annie, I am so sorry to involve you. I am glad you guys are going over to Stuart's."

Annie went to pack up her stuff, and Stuart murmured to Reggie, "You don't have to come in if you don't want to tomorrow."

"Are you kidding me? I want to come in, but Sam and I have to come up with some way to get this guy. If he wasn't so disturbed, I would do a brief spot on television about this. But that would just set him off, and he would really hurt someone. Someone must know this guy, and I hope when your team comes, Sam, they can find his prints."

Stuart gave Reggie a hug and went to Annie's.

Police arrived without any flashing lights. The officers jumped out of the truck with their kits, and followed Sam into the house. Sam returned to the front porch once officers started processing the scene.

"Maybe you should go with Annie. It really would be safer," Sam suggested to Reggie.

"I am so furious now, Sam, that I want to stay here and not leave. Besides, I am not leaving you!" Reggie felt as if she had no control of everything around her.

"Okay, you win, but let's try and relax while the men investigate. I need to let them do their work. If anyone can find prints, they can." Sam put his arms around Reggie as she hugged Lucy closer to her.

***

The Donation Man was so happy. He had single-handily shown the bitch that she couldn't mess with him.

It would not kill her to give some money. If he gave her another chance, because he really did not want to kill her, maybe she would donate. Besides, it had become fun to scare her. There was something about her he found captivating. Her spunk, her looks…he did not know, but there was something special about her. He had been careful not to leave prints, or at least he hoped he'd left nothing. Pouring ketchup on the floor had added a nice touch. They were so stupid that they did not realize he was across the street in the bushes and could see what was going on. Stupid, and cheap. Now that everyone was inside, it was time to get to the trolley stop. There were cameras, but he was careful to hide his face.

Chuckling, he almost skipped down the street.

CHAPTER 20

Reggie went to work and told Jane what had happened. Jane was so angry her body shook, and she said, "Reggie, you and Sam can stay with us."

"We might take you up on that sometime, but I really want to find out who this guy is. Enough is enough. And besides, finishing up our things today, I am going to see if there have ever been any reports of this happening to anyone in the city. The station archives may have something. I keep thinking if this has happened to me, maybe it has happened to someone else."

Later that day, after editing with Stuart and Jane, Reggie started to look through past stories. She knew Sam was at the police station going through films and seeing what the forensics guys had dug up.

She was starting to get a sore neck from sitting at the computer for so long when one reference caught her eye. Woman killed, no suspects, only the reporter's note about giving money to the poor.

"Bingo!" Reggie said as she opened the file.

She started reading the notes on the short clip dated three years earlier, and some of the reporters' notes they liked to attach with the files. Reggie turned pale, and her hands started to sweat when saw the outcome.

Woman Found Dead In Her Apartment. Forty-three-year-old Lynn Jackson was found dead with knife wounds to her stomach and carotid artery. Lynn lived with her mom and worked for a local hotel as their head of marketing.

There have been no leads or evidence at the home to lead police to the killer, but they did find a note that said, "You bitch, you should have helped out! All the rest of the people helped, but you had to be such a bitch."

Reggie saw a follow-up bit about a month later, saying there still had been no leads on who the killer was. She was shocked they had not connected the donations, but Lynn probably never went to the police like she had, and instead must have just gotten annoyed with the calls and didn't feel she was in danger.

Reggie called Sam. "Hey, Sam, I think I have something. A woman named Lynn Jackson was murdered three years ago, and judging by the note the police found, this could be the same guy. Maybe the police have some files? And see if any of the evidence connects the two."

"Sure, I would be happy to. Give me the details, Reggie." The words sunk in and Sam said, "What the hell? Did you say murdered?"

Reggie softly said, "Yes, Sam."

"Oh hell."

"I have no plans on being murdered, Sam. It might have nothing to do with my guy, but no harm in checking. And if it's our guy, then we have got to get him soon."

"You mean I have to get him soon."

"Sam, I have survived almost being killed by The Bomber, and I have no plans, as I have told you before, of dying. No crazy son of a bitch is going to kill me!"

"Let's hope not. Talk to you later. The sergeant said they were posting someone outside your place as a courtesy to me, and I'll call the detectives and give them the information you just gave me. I'll pick you up after work. Please wait there for me."

"Okay. Stuart, Jane, and I are finished, but I'll do some more work. Just give me a buzz when you're here."

"Will do. Love ya."

"Love you, too!"

As Reggie hung up the phone, she turned to see Stuart standing in the door with a look of shock on his face.

"Sorry, Reggie, but I heard what you said to Sam. I had no idea your life could really be in danger. I knew someone had broken in, but if there is a connection to a killing...."

Reggie walked over to him and touched his shoulder. "I don't want any of us to get hurt, so I'm glad you have Annie at your place until we can figure this out."

Reggie spent the rest of the afternoon getting her notes together for the documentary. When she heard the familiar bing telling her Sam had sent her a text, she opened the message and smiled. She saw a heart and "Love You" as the only message.

She was savoring a cup of coffee at her desk when her phone rang. She smiled as she thought of Sam calling to give her an update, or knowing him, just to say he loved her. Some couples didn't talk about their feelings for each other, but after being near death, both of them took every opportunity to let each other know how much they were loved. Reggie did not check the number before answering it.

"Hello, Reggie speaking."

She almost dropped the phone when she heard, "Hello, Reggie. I am glad to hear you sounding so happy now, as this would be a great time to tell me how much you want to give to my charity."

"You mean to you, don't you?" Reggie asked, not able to contain some sarcasm in her voice.

"Now, now, we don't have to be rude, Reggie. I do get a little of the money from the charity, but I have to have a salary."

Reggie looked around the office, upset with herself that she did not have her phone monitored so they would be able to trace the call. She also was upset she hadn't come up with a plan in case he called her.

"Oh, Reggie, I know you're thinking how you can trace this call, but I am too smart to use the same cell phone, and you are too dumb if you think I would."

"Was it you who trashed my place, whatever your name is?"

"You can keep calling me The Donation Man, Reggie. I think you know I am serious now, and yes, it was me who came to your place."

Reggie made the mistake of asking him, "So, what if I don't give you any money, what will you do?"

"Oh, Reggie," he said softly, "you are trying to rile me up, but in the end, you will give. Even if you don't give me money, there will be other ways you give. So let's make this simple and just give me the money I asked for."

"Let me think about it," Reggie said. "How about if you call me back in a day or two and we can talk more?" How lame, Reggie thought, he won't buy that stall.

The Donation Man chuckled and said, "I really am enjoying this game, Reggie. You know now that when you do give me the money, it won't be by mail. Okay, I will give you a day, and that will give you time to have a trap set up for me. You really don't know who you are dealing with, do you?"

Reggie didn't respond.

"I am going to hang up now, Reggie." And then he said, "And remember, this is no joke." He almost whispered the last words. "The other girl didn't give. She thought I was crazy, and that was her mistake. A deadly mistake."

There was a click, and Reggie sat down quickly as she felt slightly dizzy.

Sam strolled into the room and saw Reggie collapsed in a chair. He rushed over to her. "What happened?"

"The Donation Man called me. He basically said if I don't donate, he will hurt me in some way. He did break into the house, and he made a reference to the girl who did not give. I wanted to ask him if he meant Lynn Jackson, but decided not to say anything. I need some sort of way to let you guys hear his calls, and some way you can track me besides my cell phone if anything happens."

"Done. Let's go to the station and see what tracking devices we can use for you besides your cell phone. Your phone would be great, but this guy would probably dump it first thing if he got to you. He seems pretty smart."

Reggie's investigative reporter was starting to kick in when she thought of the woman, Lynn Jackson. "Let's see if there are any relatives we can talk to who might help us figure who Lynn talked to before she died. Maybe a dead end, but it's something. The guy's picture is out to the departments only at this point, but what if we spread it to the local news as a person of interest?"

Sam frowned, and as if weighing his words, he said, "Reggie, I know you want to get this guy, but this might make him even more agitated. Plus, we try to keep as much information out of the press as possible during an active investigation."

"But if it is released, someone might know him, and you could bring him in for questioning."

"Reggie, there are no prints to tie this guy to your break in, and we can't just pick him up and bring him in. It does not work that way."

"Okay, then let's go and speak to the relatives of the dead woman. You never know, they might ID our guy from our pictures as someone their relative knew. Can you find me the addresses, Sam, and go with me?"

"Let me clear it first," he said, making a call to the division.

Sam explained the situation, and after being given permission to go to the relative's home, he was put on hold until they got back to him and gave him the address of Lynn Jackson. He scribbled it on a pad of paper.

"Bingo," she said. "I know exactly where this house is. It is in the Garden District and not far at all. Let's go." Suddenly getting her energy back and after collecting her things, Reggie followed Sam out to his car.

CHAPTER 21

As they drove down St. Charles Avenue and past some of the beautiful mansions, Reggie reminded herself that she and Jane needed to ask one of the owners if they could highlight their home for the documentary.

They turned onto one of the gorgeous tree lined streets and found the house they were looking for. It was a classic garden house, and could have been on a poster for the Garden District.

"I think that we need to call Lynn's family before just showing up at the door. I am sorry we didn't do it back at the office, but we need to," Reggie said, feeling a sudden wave of sadness come over her for the family.

"You're right. Let me give them, a call as it's late afternoon so they may be gone. If they know I am a detective and am investigating the case, they may want to give us more details to find their daughter's killer. Let's just hope they're home."

Sam looked relieved his call was answered, and he started talking to the Jacksons.

"It's a go. They said they would talk with us now."

Even before they rang the doorbell the door opened, and in the doorway stood a woman of about sixty holding a cane, dressed up in a summer New Orleans lightweight flowing shift. She smiled, but there seemed to be a sadness behind the smile.

"Hello, I'm Mrs. Jackson. Come in, come in. I have some lemonade I can get you; or would you prefer some sweet tea?" she asked as she led them into the living room and motioned for them to sit down on the couch.

"Lemonade is fine with me," Reggie replied.

"Me too, thank you so much," Sam said.

Mrs. Jackson poured the lemonade and sat down in a big stuffed chair across from them, and began to take little sips from her crystal glass. "So, you're here about my daughter, Lynn? Has there been any progress in her case?"

Sam said, "We were not directly involved in her case, but we have been looking into it, as we think that there could be some connection to a case we are looking into now."

"Another murder?" Mrs. Jackson gasped, spilling a little of her lemonade.

"No, but we think that a person of interest we are looking at may have had some contact with your daughter," replied Reggie.

"Did your daughter get any odd phone calls prior to her death?" asked Sam.

"Odd? What do you mean by odd?" asked Mrs. Jackson.

"Well, did anyone call asking for donations from you or your daughter?" Sam asked.

"Oh, no." Suddenly Mrs. Jackson paled as she said, "Before my daughter's death she was getting very upset because she had this one man calling, or maybe it was a woman, asking for donations to their organization. She said she would give a few dollars, but the person kept saying she was richer than that, and what kind of selfish person was she. You don't think that has anything to do with her death, do you? I told the police about it, but they did not think there was any connection."

"We don't know if there is any connection for sure, but is there anything else you can tell us about this person on the phone, or how near her death the calls came?"

Seeing the look on her face made Reggie feel a pang of sadness. If it were her mom answering questions about her, if something happened, it would break her mom's heart.

"Well, Lynn worked at a hotel in the Quarter in their marketing department. She was living here with me, as my husband had passed a year earlier and she was trying to save up enough money to take her dream trip. The morning she was killed she did get a call, but I can't tell you who it was from. She looked upset, and when I asked her what was wrong, she brushed it off and said just one of those annoying calls. She got another one, but this was a text, and she really looked upset when that came. She grabbed her purse and keys and headed out the door. Before she left, she turned and said, 'Bye, Mom. I love you.' I will never forget her last words." Mrs. Jackson was getting teary eyed and pulled out a tissue to wipe her eyes.

"Would you mind if we pulled your daughter's phone records and see if there is anything that may help us?" Sam asked softly.

"No, but you need to tell me more about what is going on now first," Mrs. Jackson replied.

Reggie spoke up. "I am getting calls from some man who keeps getting angrier and angrier that I am not donating to his charity. He has pushed me and broken into my apartment. We don't know if it is the same man, but that's why we are checking it out."

Mrs. Jackson stood up and went over to Reggie, took Reggie's hand, and looked into her eyes. "You be careful. If this is the person who murdered my wonderful daughter, you are in danger. Look through any records you want, and I hope we can catch my daughter's killer. It won't bring Lynn back, but it will stop another parent from going through the pain of having a child, no matter if they are an adult, die."

Reggie found herself squeezing the woman's hand gently, saying, "We will try hard to find your daughter's killer, and I will be careful. Thanks for seeing us."

As they walked to the door, they saw the portrait of Lynn and her mom near the entrance. Sam squeezed Reggie's hand briefly, knowing that besides being afraid, she was just a woman who got upset seeing others in pain.

"Beautiful picture of you two," Reggie said.

"Thanks," Mrs. Jackson said softly. "That was taken a few months before she died, so I keep it there to see her every day."

As they stepped onto the porch, Reggie felt herself getting angry. "Let's go get those phone records," Reggie said, her sadness turning into a fierce determination to catch the monster if he had killed Lynn. "We can have pizza and review them if you're game. Jane and I have another interview to do tomorrow, so let's do it tonight."

***

Sam grinned at Reggie. She was a very determined woman, and that was one of the many things he loved about her. She had no idea that he had gotten a ring before visiting and had planned on proposing to her. He had almost lost her once before, and although a ring was a ring, for him it meant that he wanted to spend every day with her, to hear her laugh, see her get annoyed, hold hands with her, and feel her body pressed to his. Now wasn't the time to propose, but he would soon.

CHAPTER 22

Sam and Reggie settled into the spare office at the police station with their pizza and began the process of looking at Lynn's calls. It was the text that they really wanted. If it was The Donation Man, he probably used a burner phone, but at least they would see what he said.

It took a while, but finally they found what they were looking for.

"Bingo, we have the text," Sam said, staring at the computer.

"What does it say?" Reggie asked excitedly, looking over Sam's shoulder.

"Wow, this guy is really something," he said. "He said he was sorry that he made her so angry and that he really was just doing his work. He wanted to make it up to her and meet her someplace for coffee."

"What did she say?"

"She never responded, but he kept sending her more, and on the last one she said she was going to go to the police to show them her phone, so they would know what he was doing," Sam said. "But his last text was, and I quote, 'I was right, you are a bitch, and you'll be sorry.'"

Reggie shuddered. "I looked again into the detective's notes, and there was no phone found on her body or around her."

"It must be him, Reggie, and we have got to get this guy soon before he gets you!"

Reggie didn't say anything for a while, but then said slowly, "How about when he calls again, I get him to meet me somewhere? You could have me tailed, and we could catch him. At least we can get his prints and find out who this guy is."

"Reggie, we have no evidence to prove this guy is doing anything wrong. He left no prints. He had a burner phone. All we have is his face at the scene of things, and even when you were pushed he knew where to do it so it would not show clearly on camera. Even if he was in the area or was near your place, there still has to be proof. I guess we could bring him in as a person of interest, but if he walks, he is really going to come hard at you."

"But you guys would be close. He knows I may wear a bug, but can't you come up with something that is so small, like a pinpoint camera and mic, that he would never suspect?"

"I do not want to use you as bait, and that is settled," Sam said. His upper lip tightened like it did when he was worried or annoyed.

"I know you're worried, but it is my life, and I don't want this guy hurting me either. Use me as bait, but for God's sake give me the stuff so you can get this bastard! At least let me get one of the guys here to go over what I may be able to use after you talk to the captain and fill him in on this. If he is totally against the idea, I will reconsider, but I don't feel we have any choice. He is going to try to kill me no matter what. I don't even know that if I said I would give money it would make a difference at this point."

"Oh shit," Sam sighed. "Why on earth did I get involved with such a bull-headed reporter?"

Reggie could see Sam was really upset and worried about her. Her tone softened as she said to him, "I will be really careful. There is no way I want to get hurt and leave you, Sam. In fact, my life is wonderful with you, and that's why I want this maniac out of the way so we can forget all this." Reggie tried to ease the tension by joking as she continued, "Two attempts at my life, one a year. Hey, what is it about me?"

Sam's tight shoulders relaxed and he drew her

into his arms and said, "What is it about you that makes people want to kill you?" He kissed her gently on her forehead. "Like it or not, I am going to do everything to protect you, Miss Independent. Now let me go talk to the captain, as he is still here, and see what he says. If it is a go, then we can meet tomorrow after work or before and put the device on you. This guy said he was going to call you tomorrow, so we have to have some plan. Let me take a few pieces of pizza to the captain, too."

Sam left the office and returned with the captain. He walked over to Reggie and looked her in the eyes as he said, "I'm not thrilled with putting you in danger, but if there is a connection to the other homicide then we want this guy stopped now! Who knows how many more women this guy could have done this to?"

"Who knows how many more women this guy could have killed," Reggie said in a low serious, almost sad tone.

"I will have Les meet with you in the morning, but let's have him meet with you somewhere other than here. He may have seen you tonight, but let's have Les meet you somewhere you would go normally," the captain said.

"I will be working tomorrow, so how about my office? Jane has to go out of town for a family reunion, so this is a perfect time. She will be gone, and I won't have to worry about her safety."

"That will work out great. But what about tonight?" ask the captain.

"I am going to be at her place, and believe me, no one is going to get in," said Sam.

Reggie added, "After last year, I do know how to shoot a gun if I need to, and I have baseball bats."

"We can also put a patrol car near your house, but an unmarked one so this guy does not get scared away," the captain said.

"Sounds great," Reggie said. "I'm glad my neighbor is at Stuart's."

"I would feel better if a car were there at night, because I don't want him going after her," added Sam.

"I need to see Stuart and Annie and tell them all that is going on, or even better, stop at Stuart's place after a call and fill him in," added Reggie.

Reggie felt her heart racing as she thought back to The Bomber last year and how sure the FBI and police had been that she and Maggie were protected. That was until the maniac found a way to find them and hunt them. She now knew after her and Sam being shot that there was no guarantee they were safe.

The captain warned them both to be careful, and

they left for Stuart's.

Stuart had a beautiful place, one Reggie knew he had hoped he and his fiancée would share before she dumped him. They rang the doorbell and got a surprised Stuart at the door.

"Is everything okay?" Stuart asked, at the same time motioning for them to come inside.

"Lots to fill you in on, and Annie, too," replied Reggie.

"You guys want some dinner? I was just cooking Annie my special pasta."

Reggie rubbed her belly. "Sounds great, but we are full of pizza. We won't stay long, but we need to tell both you and Annie what is going on."

"You look too serious. Why am I starting to get nervous about all this?" Annie said, coming around the corner frowning, having heard what was said.

They all sat down, and Stuart gave them a beer as they began their story. The room was almost dead silent when they finished telling Annie and Stuart what had gone on. Annie was biting her bottom lip, as Reggie knew she did when she got nervous.

"I am so sorry you had to be involved in this, but we want to keep you safe. The best place for you both to be is here and not near the house," said Reggie.

Surprised, Annie said, "I can't keep staying here. Stuart, you have been great, but I probably should go home."

Stuart moved closer to Annie on the couch and said, "Don't worry. I have plenty of room here, and you're welcome to use the spare room again. We should go back to get some of your things and you have your laptop, and you can get your box of important papers and stay here as long as you need to."

"Okay, guys, how about if Annie comes back with us and we will bring her back, but we will use back roads and be sure that we are not being followed. We don't even know if this guy has a car or if he gets around by the streetcar," said Sam. "We will bring her back here tonight, and she will have her things. I would like to tell you that this is only going to go on for a few days, but if this guy is the same one that killed Lynn Jackson, he could be a very dangerous man."

"Okay, let's go now," Annie said, quickly standing up. "I'm trying to be positive. Besides, I have to get back for this wonderful dinner Stuart is cooking me."

Stuart gave a slight grin at Annie's comment, and Reggie, even with all that was going on, felt there was a connection happening with the two of them.

They headed back to Reggie's and went next door to gather up Annie's things. This was one time Annie was glad she did not have any pets at home, as she would have been sick to leave them. Sam checked out both places before letting them in, and watched for cars, or people walking, to make sure The Donation Man was not around.

After they had gone back and dropped Annie off, they went back home. Reggie thought she would be exhausted from all the day's events, but once they were inside and Sam had checked out the place to make sure the house was safe, she went over to him and wrapped her arms around him, pulled his head closer to hers, and started to kiss him passionately on the mouth. She felt her body getting hot as she kissed him with a sense of urgency. She grabbed his hand and pulled him up the stairs, continuing her kisses, feeling her body ignite as they fell onto the bed. They urgently tore off each other's clothes and lay naked in the moonlight. Their kisses got more intense, and the buildup of desire left them with only intermittent breaths until they each let out a low moan as they came in a wave of passion.

***

In another part of town in a small apartment.

"Oh!" The Donation Man laughed. They probably thought he was waiting around the corner for him to attack. Little did they know that he liked the chase and fear and wanted this to go on longer. They would be shocked to know he had a real job, and today was a day he had to work

all day and most of the night. Just a regular guy who joked with his coworkers, went to bars, and went home to his perfect home. The donation money was just a way to earn some more bucks…and besides, it was fun when someone said no. He had it set up so they could not trace the money and people once they gave. Most forgot about it, even for taxes. People were dumb, but he was clever. Hadn't his family said he was too clever for his own good growing up? But he was not the one that was the fool, they were.

He was also a master of disguises from his days in plays, and that came in handy these days. So he would sleep like a baby, and he hoped Reggie and her stupid boyfriend detective would be on guard all night and toss and turn. She should have been nicer, and tomorrow when he called her, he would tell her that. He had tried to tell the other woman that, but did she listen? No, and look where that got her.

CHAPTER 23

Les was waiting for Reggie at her office when she and Sam came in. He was a short round man with glasses, and carried a case that he opened on the desk once Reggie and Sam closed the door. He did not crack a smile but began pulling out equipment, giving Reggie instructions on the pinpoint camera and trying to find the best place to put it on her. He could have put it on her blouse as a pin, but if this guy was really smart, he would guess that right away. Les prided himself on using the newest equipment for recording people, and this one was easy to attach to anything. The question for him was where this guy would not see it. What if he had her put away her purse or cell phone, and where could they get good audio and visual feeds?

"I think the best place would be as an earring. The pair I have in mind look like ones you would wear anyway, and if you can keep your hair behind your ear, we would get great sound of him and an audio," Les said, pulling out two from a small pouch.

"That might work," Reggie said. "I wear pierced earrings all the time, so he might never notice. I don't understand how they pick up the audio. Do I wear a wire?"

Les for the first time cracked a smile. "Absolutely not. This is really high tech stuff that can pick up the audio. Not many people know about it, but it is my job to use the newest out there."

Sam said, "But what if he does find them? What then?"

"We have plan B in place, Sam," Les said. "I am going to put another audio on her jacket pocket, and it will look like a button only. They make them so they can stick on and look like part of her jacket."

"That is fine and good, and I know I am getting nervous," Reggie said, "but who is going to be listening to all this in case this guy goes ballistic?"

"I will be listening during this time, but you are going to arrange to meet this guy in a public place so he doesn't go ballistic on you," Les said, trying to reassure her.

"But he did hurt me in two very public places in the city. What is to stop him from doing it again?"

"This time we are listening, and you will have an

undercover guy when we do this, just in case," Les replied.

"I will be the undercover guy," Sam said.

"Not a good idea," Les said, frowning and shaking his head no. "This guy has seen you, and you would tip him off right away. I have my guys on my team that even the captain would not recognize when they are in disguise. I will assign someone."

"What if he is nice and doesn't say anything?" Reggie was growing more nervous with each passing thought and comment.

"That is what Sam and I will coach you on now, before he calls again and you set up a place. I would suggest the Quarter because there are lots of people, but you must find a quiet place so we can see and hear you. How about the coffee shop at the edge of The Quarter you mentioned? Quiet, yet easy to get to."

"Now, you just have to hope he will call you today as he said he would," Sam said.

"Let's begin the 'what if' scenarios," Les interjected.

They went over and over lines with Reggie, which should have made her more at ease, but Reggie felt her chest tighten and got a little queasy in the stomach at the reality of how she could get hurt or even killed by this guy. Reggie tried to be calm and have all they said sink in. She knew she could do this, but that didn't take away her anxiety.

"Ready, Reggie?" Sam asked, gently touching her shoulder, knowing her so well to know she was scared to death and trying to be brave. "Hey, don't worry if you're nervous," Sam continued. "I still get nervous about things like this I have to do with the department. In fact, it's good to be a little nervous, because it makes you more cautious and aware of your surroundings. And besides, we will be there for you. The guys will be listening here, and you'll have someone assigned to you, too. We will get this guy, Reggie."

Just as if The Donation Man had heard what they were saying, Reggie's phone rang. The three of them looked at each other, a bit startled. Reggie froze for a few seconds, but Sam nodded for her to pick up.

"Hello, Reggie speaking."

"Hello, Reggie." The Donation Man's voice was a calm and soft, even voice. "I know you couldn't sleep last night because you had been waiting for my call. It's funny that we're getting closer now, and you must think of me a lot. I know I think of you a lot, Reggie," he said, in an almost flirty low, guttural voice.

"What do you want?" Reggie asked, trying to be kind instead of yelling at him what an asshole he was.

"I want you to donate to my cause. That is all I have ever wanted, till now. But since you have been so stingy, I want you to donate to my cause and to apologize to me."

Reggie hadn't expected that part of the deal, but improvised when she said, "I am so sorry I didn't give to your cause, but I give to a lot of causes, and I had to draw the line somewhere."

"That is not a very good apology, Reggie," The Donation Man said, his tone sounding less pleasant. "Try again."

Les and Sam were trying to trace the call, and Sam wrote a few key words down for Reggie to say to The Donation Man.

"I am sorry, and I am sorry that you almost hurt me. I never meant for anything like this to happen. Let me give you some money now. How can I get it to you?"

There was a long pause and a sudden sinister chuckle. "Oh yes, I will give you my address, and you can send it to me. Are you goddamn kidding me? I will meet you somewhere, and you can give me the money. If you bring anyone, or I sense any setup, you truly will be sorry. Nice lady you work with, and I bet she has a family, too. And what a nice neighbor you have. Don't screw with me, lady."

"I'm not," Reggie said sincerely. "I just want to give you your money and forget this ever happened!" Reggie really meant it when she said she wanted to put all this behind her.

"Okay," The Donation Man said after a while. "Where do you want to meet?"

"How about the coffee shop on the edge of The Quarter, the one that—"

"First of all, I am no fool. I do not want to meet there, but let's meet at the one two blocks away on the corner. I know what you look like, so go in and get a table. They have no surveillance in there, so you can tell your lover boy not to get his hopes up. I plan on never being caught, especially by some dumb female and her cop boyfriend."

Reggie was furious, but calmly said, "Fine, we will meet there at three, and don't you bring anyone either."

"What?" The Donation Man said, sounding shocked. "I don't need anyone to help me do what I do, so don't worry, I am all yours and yours alone." She could almost hear a grin through the phone. The Donation Man continued. "See you later, Reggie. And I hope you're wearing something that will turn me on."

Then there was silence.

Reggie shivered, and Sam came over to hug her.

"He has never said anything sexual like that before. That just creeps me out, Sam," Reggie said with disgust.

"Makes me mad," Sam replied, his jaw tightening and his fists clenching.

"Okay, let's get everything in order. It will take you about ten minutes to walk to the coffee shop, and you don't want to be late. He did not tell you how much you are to donate, but let's give him an envelope with $200 in it. If that satisfies him, he will take it and leave, and hopefully when he leaves, we put a bulletin out with his picture from the pin."

"Sam," Reggie said. "I don't think I ever asked if Lynn was sexually assaulted. Was she?"

Les and Sam glanced at each other, and then Sam looked directly into Reggie's eyes. "Yes, she was."

"Then there is DNA evidence on this guy?" asked Reggie.

"Yes and no. There is evidence, but no one matched the DNA in any of the systems," replied Les.

"Damn!" Reggie said. "Well, this guy is not going to sexually assault or kill me." She felt herself getting furious at this predator. "Now, Les, get me all setup. I will leave here around 2:30. I know it sounds corny, and I trust you guys, but I really want to call my folks to say hi. I won't tell them this is going on. But if this goes sour, I just need to talk to them again."

"Reggie...." Sam paled. "This is not going to go sour. It is not!"

"I know, but it would make me feel better." She smiled at him, knowing Sam could not bear the thought that anything could happen to her.

Reggie left the room and gave her folks a call. Her dad answered and said, "Wait a minute, Reggie, let me get your mom on the phone, too." She could hear her dad calling her mom through the phone. "Angie, Reggie's on the phone!" They had a back room with two land lines, as they still felt they could hear better than with their smartphone.

"Hi honey," her mom said, sounding so happy she'd called. "What's new?"

"Oh, nothing much," Reggie lied, trying to spare her parents' worry. "I just wanted to call and tell you that New Orleans has been a blast, but I miss you guys. Maybe I can fly up for a weekend and see you both? I know you talked about coming here, and that would be great, but I miss home and would like our next visit to be up there, if it's okay?"

"That would be great," her parents said at the same time. "We miss you too. Just let us know when you want to come up, and we will arrange our schedule at the ice cream shop to see you. We may have you help for a few hours, but at least we will all be laughing together."

Reggie felt herself calm down as she pictured being with her folks. She really did miss them, and felt guilty it took worrying about being killed to really miss them even more.

"We also want you to sample our new ice cream creation," her dad said.

"Okay, what is it?" Reggie laughed, as her parents were always inventing new flavors.

"We're calling it 'The Reggie,'" her mom replied.

"Yeah, sure. Really, though, what is this one?" asked Reggie.

"'The Reggie,' no kidding. We thought that we would make one and combine your favorite flavors. It's a hit, and we get to tell all the tourists about you and brag," her mom replied.

"You guys...." Reggie actually started giggling, feeling such a warmth towards her parents. She wanted to tell them she wished she could hug them once more, or how much she appreciated all they had done for her and that she adored them, but the "I miss you and love you" would have to do. They chatted for a few more minutes, and finally she said, "Gotta go. I'll call you next weekend to see about coming up. This time I'll come up alone, but I do want Sam to come up and visit too sometime."

"Ah, getting serious about that fine young man,

are you?" her mom asked. "For what it's worth, your dad and I like him a lot. We were sorry to have met him in the hospital when you two got shot by The Bomber, but he's nice. No more hospital visits, though, okay, Reggie?" her mom said. "How about something fun, like a wedding instead?"

"Oh, Mom," Reggie sighed, glad to not have to comment on the hospital remark, but her mom and dad would love it if she married Sam. "Gotta go, really."

"Love you, honey, and remember to be careful," her dad said.

"Will do," Reggie said, hanging up.

Reggie sat very still for about five minutes, got up and walked into the room, and said, "Okay, guys, let's do this. Let's get that bastard."

CHAPTER 24

Reggie glanced at herself in the mirror. She hoped her earring looked natural enough to blend in with the other one and draw no attention. She smoothed her hair, put it behind her ear on the microphone side, practiced her smile, and walked out of the bathroom knowing she may fool The Donation Man. She would never fool Sam. The sooner they got this over, the better.

There was a man standing next to Les and Sam. "Reggie, this is Tom. He is going to be the extra eyes we need on you besides Sam, and I'll be here monitoring the device you're wearing," said Les.

"Hi, Tom," Reggie said, shaking his hand. "So you're the man who will have my back?"

"Hi, Reggie, and yes, I am going to be within a few feet of you. If this guy spots me, it will be a bust, but I am hoping I don't look like a cop today," replied Tom.

Tom was about five feet eight inches tall, built very solid, and had his share of tattoos. Dressed in a tank, shorts, and sandals, he was unshaven, and his eyes looked bloodshot. Reggie hoped it wasn't from drinking, but knew he probably put something in his eyes to keep up the ruse of being just another tourist wanting to have a little fun on a hot day in New Orleans.

"How you are going to hide?" Reggie asked Tom.

"I'm going to be in the bar a few doors down and across from where you're at. I am going to follow you at a safe distance, carrying my pralines bag to look the tourist part. I'll be sipping on a drink at the place, but where I can see you."

"But how can you see me if I am inside?" Reggie gave Tom an uncertain look, not sure she liked this idea.

"I am counting on these guys to be your inside ears, and the minute you step out the door, I will take action. I don't want to grab him going in because we don't want this guy to walk if we have nothing on him. As you said before, if he walks, he is going to be one angry fellow. We also don't know if he is going to be in disguise like me or look like himself," said Tom.

"I would feel better if I carried my pepper spray

like I usually do. Plus, will I be able to have my cell phone?" Reggie asked, knowing most likely that would be the case.

"Yes, carry those, but be careful when you pull out the money. You don't want him to see the spray," Les interjected.

"Now it's time," Sam said. "You'll be fine, Reggie."

Sam gave her a big yet soothing hug, and for a minute held her so close she could smell the faint odor of coconut shampoo in his hair. Reggie wanted to believe him, but last year, Detective Mike had assured her before she got shot by The Bomber. She could hear him saying that she and Maggie were safe and The Bomber would not find them. She took a deep breath, looked into Sam's eyes, and told herself he wouldn't let anything happen to her.

"Okay, I'm off," she said, stepping out of her office and heading to the building's front entrance, and into the hot New Orleans sun.

The tourists were heavy and the music loud. Reggie listened to it as she walked, and it calmed her down somewhat. She let the music tell her it would all be okay. She was a little nervous this maniac would try to kill her as she headed to meet him, but she knew in her gut he wanted to talk to her in person, and mostly scare her.

She saw the coffee shop ahead and no one standing outside. She checked her cell phone to see the time; it was five minutes to three. She entered the coffee shop, which had dim light, and looked around. There was no one there except a few couples. Reggie ordered herself a coffee and sat at one of the tables, in the middle of the restaurant, knowing somehow The Donation Man would be mad if she sat by a window or too close to the front door.

After waiting ten minutes and trying not to play with her button, she saw a man enter the coffee shop and place an order. He had a very short buzz cut, dark glasses, and a blue T-shirt. No one would remember him, as he looked like tons of other people in The Quarter. She did not know if this was him for sure, but there was one thing that said it was— the goddamn air of cockiness. When he turned, the larger lower lip gave him away.

Reggie felt tense. She wanted to yell into the mic, but she knew she had to play things out and let the police do their job.

After getting his coffee, the man walked over to the table. "Why, aren't you that reporter I see on television?" he asked, trying to sound surprised to see her having coffee in this little shop.

For a moment, Reggie was confused, but said, "Why yes, I am."

"Then I must sit for a moment, if you don't mind," he said, giving her a warm smile as he sat down beside her, and placed two pieces of paper on the table

Reggie stared at his face as he adjusted his chair and casually started sipping his coffee. He had intense brown eyes, a slight dimple on his chin, and when he looked at her, she felt he could read her every thought. If she did not know he was crazy, she would have seen why girls could be attracted to him.

She pushed the envelope to him and said, "I am sorry I did not donate. Here is the money for you."

"The money you choose to donate, you mean?" he asked, frowning slightly.

"Yes, the money that I want to donate."

The Donation Man left the envelope on the table, and very carefully turned over a piece of paper. In bold letters it said, DO NOT SAY A WORD, I KNOW YOU'RE WIRED SOMEHOW. NOW FOLLOW ME. Reggie shook her head no, but he turned over the second piece of paper, and there was a picture of Annie. Under her photo it said, I HAVE HER. DON'T TRY ANYTHING STUPID. IF YOU SAY ONE WORD, I WILL KILL HER OR SOMEONE I KNOW WILL.

Reggie's hands started to shake, and she quickly tried to think of all her options. *Talk into the mic and he may bolt, and then Annie could be in danger. Go with him and maybe be killed.* She had to save Annie, and knew Sam would hear the transmissions on her jacket. She got up from the chair as The Donation Man stood.

The Donation Man gently felt her arms and body and reached his hands over to her jacket lapel, almost in a caress, fondling her button in his hand. Next he touched her earring. He smiled, his lips becoming even fuller, and his eyes smiled too, almost as if he was saying, "Gotcha." He scribbled for her to take off all her jewelry and put it in her purse.

He began to take off her jacket, putting his finger on her lips. Loudly he said, "No, I want you to read this. It will take about ten minutes, but it explains why I collect money. I don't want you to say a word, just read."

The Donation Man then swiftly put Reggie in front of him and directed her to the back of the coffee shop, where he hung her purse and jacket on a hook and then led her outside into the back street. He handed her a blonde wig from his bag and motioned for her to put it on, as well as a silk shirt over her blouse. There were a few people near there, but Reggie and The Donation Man drew no attention. Just another attractive couple walking in The Quarter.

Reggie figured it would take about five more minutes before Sam and Les realized what was going on, which would be too late to have Tom follow her. He was across the street, and would be the first one to run into the shop. If she had been thinking faster, she would have dropped something.

Damn, her pepper spray and phone were in her purse. They would find the purse and know she was in danger, but unless they could track them by webcams, she was definitely in trouble. Oh, God, she thought. Oh, God. She did have the wrinkled up napkin in her pocket that she had played with when full of nerves in the coffee shop before he came in, but that was it.

He led her down one block and motioned, after opening the door, for her to get in a small tan car parked on the street. What he failed to see was that she had not put both earrings in the purse, but carefully held one in her fist and dropped it to the ground out of his sight.

Once in, he said sternly, "Don't try anything funny or your friend is in trouble. I am the only one who knows where she is, and if you pull anything, she will never be found!"

Reggie nodded her head to show she understood, and buckled her seat belt. With the blonde wig, sunglasses, and a different colored blouse, she knew that even on the webcams she might not be recognized.

"Didn't think I had a car, did you? You think I am some psycho. But to all my friends, I am an ordinary guy. I know you hope the back of the coffee shop would have cameras, but they don't. I checked that out before we met, and I am surprised your stupid cop boyfriend did not look into that."

Reggie just stared out the front window trying to keep herself from shaking all over. She didn't want to give The Donation Man the satisfaction of seeing her scared.

"Really, a wire in a button. Wow, you guys really do think I am crazy or just dumb," The Donation Man chuckled. He was so sure of himself that he didn't even lock the doors. He seemed to know Reggie would not let her friend down. "Now you just relax. It will take us about ten minutes to get to where we are going. If people see me with you, they'll think I have a pretty blonde girlfriend that I'm taking to my home. I told the neighbors I was having a stay in the city vacation, so they'll chuckle and say 'Good old boy bringing a cutie home for some fun.'"

Reggie didn't think anything he had in mind was going to be fun. She just needed to stay calm so she could save her friend.

"Some fun we are going to have. Actually, I am glad you did not donate." He brushed Reggie's leg with his hand softly, and she felt herself shudder.

148

CHAPTER 25

After about five minutes of restaurant noise and no conversation, Les and Sam gave each other a concerned look.

"Something feels wrong," Sam said to Les.

"Come on, Tom," Les said into the radio. "We have not heard anything. Something feels wrong. Go to the shop and tell us what you see."

"Copy," came Tom's reply through the radio.

About two minutes later, they heard Tom, his words drenched with despondency. "Nothing, I see nothing. She is not here. I am going to go into the bathrooms and storerooms. Stay on the line, and I'll tell you what I see."

"Oh God," Sam moaned, suddenly feeling as if his world was crashing down. "Reggie, for God's sake, be okay."

"Okay guys, I've checked the bathrooms and she

149

is not there, but there are hooks outside the bathrooms for coats or things, so let me check that." After a few minutes, Tom said, "Got it. Found out why we did not hear anything but background noise. Her jacket is hung up with the pin on it, and under the jacket is her purse with the pepper spray. He must have ordered her to hang it up

"Looks like our guy is too smart and got her out of there without us knowing it," replied Les.

"Oh shit!" Sam said, jumping up and bolting to the door. "I have got to go there and see if anyone saw anything. Les, can you get the feed from around there and see what this guy looks like now?"

"Sure, just go. You and Tom can take it from here."

As Sam ran to the coffee shop, he found himself angry, afraid, and mad at himself that he could not keep the woman he loved safe. Screw that she was independent, she still was the woman he loved, and now The Donation Man had her.

He entered the shop and saw Tom was talking to what looked to be the manager and a waiter.

"Yeah, I saw this attractive lady sitting there, and a man joined her. I did not see anything that looked suspicious, but I did notice them head to the back door. I figured they must be regulars, because not everyone knows we have a back door. Sorry, but I don't have any cameras. Used to, but the one we had went out yesterday."

Damn, Sam scolded himself. Why didn't they check that before they had Reggie meet The Donation Man?

Sam asked Tom to get prints off the back door and asked the manager to lock it. He went out the back door and looked around the street. There was enough room that someone could easily park their car by the coffee shop. He did not think The Donation Man had a car, but he checked the area anyway.

The only space that was empty was almost directly in front of the shop. He looked around to see if there were any cameras on any of the businesses or any cameras on the alley corners. Nothing that he saw, but he would check with Les and see if anyone had one that The Donation Man did not know about that might have been trained on the spot. God, he felt stupid. He should have been more thorough.

His eye caught something shiny on the ground, and he stooped down to get it. In his fingers was a small pierced earring...Reggie's. Knowing Reggie, she took it out to leave a clue, let them know she had been taken somewhere in a car. *That's my Reggie*, he thought. *Help us find you.*

Tom came out of the shop. "I got a description of the man with Reggie, and one of the employees actually was outside when they went out back. He said the woman seemed to know the man, and she went into the passenger seat without a struggle. The car was a tan sedan, local plates, which looked to be about ten years old. Nothing too noticeable about it; he remembered it had a bumper sticker on the back, but he couldn't remember what it said. It had some large design, which he could draw for us. He did not remember the plate number, though."

"We have got to get back to the station and have your computer expert, besides Les, check the city cameras and see where they are headed. If Reggie left this clue, maybe there is something else that might lead us to the guy," said Sam.

CHAPTER 26

Reggie didn't have a blindfold on as they drove out of town. She was not that familiar with the city, so she did not know where they were except that they had left downtown and were headed towards a more remote location out in a parish she didn't know.

He pulled into a small ranch home that had lots of land. There were other homes nearby, but each private because of all the tall foliage. The house, from what she could tell, had one of the privacy fences that was six feet high and a sign saying, "Beware of the dog."

"You have a dog?" she asked casually, trying to not aggravate him by making small talk.

"No, but it sure makes people wonder if I do, and keeps strangers off my property," he said. "Now, when we get out, I expect no funny business. Not that any neighbors can see, but act like you are just a

153

girlfriend of mine. Hold my hand once I get you out of the car." He slowly smiled and pulled out a small gun, pointing it right at her. "I know I won't have to use this, but I don't want you to think that I won't. Now, I'll come around and get you."

"Where is Annie?" Reggie asked, cringing at the thought of holding his hand.

"Let's get in the house, and I will let you know where your friend is once we're in there. You probably want to see that she is okay. Just continue to be a good girl, and I will let you talk to her."

Reggie tried to take in as much as she could about the house and street, but she had a sinking feeling if he had not blindfolded her, he might have no thought of ever returning her to her home. And when he pulled out the gun, her heart sank at the idea that Annie might be dead already. She started to feel faint but willed herself to keep focused, and there would be some way she could beat this maniac at his game.

He came around and opened the door ever so gently, helping her out of the car. As he walked her up the walk, Reggie wished she had something of hers to drop into the flower bed. At least if something were to happen to her, it would be proof she was there. It made her suddenly sad to be thinking like this, but she knew she must.

He opened the door to the house. As soon as they entered, he put in the code to the alarm, first turning her around so she did not see the numbers he put in. She counted five numbers, and saw the last two numbers being pushed in the reflection of the grandfather clock pressed up against the wall.

As soon as he deactivated the alarm, he told her to wait, and he armed it again.

"Can't let you get out now, can we?" he said, still not realizing she could see him pressing the buttons; or he could, and just wanted to tease her.

She saw the first number, five, the second number was three, and she had the last two, but there was one missing.

The place looked like many homes she had been in. At the entrance was a foyer, to the right was the dining room, to the left the living room, and down the hall must be the kitchen and bedrooms.

The furniture in the living room was done in tans and blacks, and everything seemed in perfect order. Too perfect, she thought. There were pictures on the walls, but they were all in dark colors. There were no personal touches except for a beautiful wooden box on the coffee table, and a basket filled with newspapers by the couch.

Looking to her right and into the dining room, Reggie saw a beautiful wood table with four chairs, a cabinet with some glasses and trophies in it, and fresh flowers in the center in a cut glass vase.

Again, the pictures on the wall were dark and serious, and the carpet looked like it had never been stepped on. All perfect.

As she walked by both rooms with The Donation Man, him not letting her stop to glance in, she tried to see if there was anything she could use to defend herself if she needed to. Nothing, except the cut glass vase she had seen on the dining room table.

As they walked into the family room, she saw another sectional couch, a coffee table, and a green marble fireplace with built in bookcases. The bookshelves were filled with books and a few pictures, which she was too far away to see. She did not think this wacko had a family, but who knew.

He directed her into the kitchen off the family room, and told her to sit at the wood table. In front of her were a paper plate and cup. As she quickly glanced around the kitchen, she saw no dishes, pans, or anything out of the cupboards she could use as a weapon.

"Where is my friend?" Reggie demanded as soon as she was seated.

"Now is that any way for a guest to treat me in my home? You will see your friend soon, so just sit and eat what I have fixed you."

He opened the refrigerator, all the while making sure Reggie sat in the chair. She was tempted to jump up and run for the door, but she wanted to see where Annie was first. Besides, he still had the gun with him, and there was something about him that made her think he would have no qualms about shooting her because he had no qualms about stabbing the other woman, Lynn.

He pulled out a plastic tub of chicken salad and a croissant. He used a plastic spoon to put it on the sandwiches, and gave her one with a few chips, as well as a plastic bottle of soda.

"Now isn't this nice?" he asked, actually sounding happy.

"Yes, thank you," Reggie said, trying to sound as sincere as possible.

The Donation Man ate his sandwich very quickly while standing up, and just kept staring at her as she ate hers. Reggie knew she had to be more personal with him, and maybe she'd stand a chance of getting away. If she got him talking, she would have time to glance around more and see ways to escape. She wished the days of having landlines weren't over for many, as she did not have her cell phone and he must have his somewhere on him.

"I know you're trying to figure out how to get out. You can set off the alarm and go out, but I will get you before you get to the door. I have a gun, and your poor friend if you decide to run. Your poor, dear friend."

"Why don't you just let me go, leave town, and go where you won't be found?"

"Are you fucking kidding me?" he asked, his face starting to turn red. "Leave town. I don't think so. Who in the hell are you to tell me what to do? Just like my mom. She told me what to do all the time. So just shut up!"

They were both silent for a moment, and then The Donation Man said in a soft voice, "Oh, Reggie, I am sorry I got mad at you. But from now on, I know we will get along. The other girl could have had it good, but she wanted nothing to do with me. With us, it will be different."

Reggie sat still as he gently took a napkin, wiped his mouth, and threw the plates away. He wiped every single crumb off the table and sat down across from her.

"I bet you want to know how I turned into such an interesting man, Reggie."

Reggie wanted to say, "I could care less," but there was part of her that wanted to know. "After you show me Annie and I see she is okay, then you can tell me your whole life story."

He shook his head and sighed. "Oh, Reggie, what

am I going to do with you? Okay, we can talk later. Let me show you, Annie. Come this way."

He got up and gently helped her up, then escorted her down a hallway off the kitchen where she saw two bedrooms on her left. At the end of the hall they came to a large bedroom that must have been the master. It also looked to be in perfect order. The bed was a queen bed with a beautiful black and white quilt on it. A beautiful chair was in the room, and very colorful oil paintings all over the walls. This didn't look like the rest of the house with the color, but it was in perfect order. What was out of place was a plastic table and two chairs at one corner of the room.

"Come in, Reggie, look around more. Don't worry, I am not going to try to seduce you, but I do want you to see this room."

"Where is Annie?" Reggie demanded, yet almost pleaded with The Donation Man.

The Donation Man actually smiled as he said, "You're right, Reggie, I have kept you from her too long. Follow me." He pressed a button placed in the center of one of his statues, and like in the movies a door in the wall opened. "She's in here, Reggie."

Reggie raced into the room, where she saw another small bedroom with a mini refrigerator. It was also perfect and decorated in pastels, and had a bookcase that was filled with books and magazines. "Where is Annie?" Reggie asked, feeling angry and confused.

She left the bedroom and headed into the small bathroom that had a toilet, a tiny stand-up shower, and sink, but no mirror. Still not seeing Annie, she heard the slam of a heavy door. Running into the bedroom, she found that the door had been shut. Panicked, she quickly crossed the room and pulled on the handle. Nothing. It was locked. The door was thick and probably soundproof.

"What the hell are you doing?" she screamed. Looking at the door for a keyhole or something, she found nothing but a small intercom beside it. She'd had one of these when growing up, so she pressed the button that said talk. "What is going on?"

"Oh, Reggie, I did think you were smarter than this. What is going on is that your friend Annie is safe and sound at your boss's place, and you are here with me in my guest room. No one will ever find you."

"Let me out now! You can't keep me here. Sam will find me or someone will!" she said, furious more than scared now.

"Oh, I don't think so. You're talking through the intercom, but I am more high-tech than that. I can see you on my laptop, but you can't see me. I can hear you without you pressing the button, but I thought it would be fun to test you."

"You bastard!" Reggie said, then instantly regretted saying that. She must keep a rapport and not make him angry.

"Not very nice. What would your news listeners think if they heard you talking like that, Reggie?"

Reggie took a deep breath and said slowly, "I am sorry. I am just upset. I don't know why you are doing this and I am scared."

There was silence.

"Did you hear me?" Reggie asked.

There was no answer, just deep breathing.

"You have everything you need in there. I have to go out."

"Oh, no," Reggie moaned. "Let me out!"

There was nothing as Reggie pounded on the door. Finally, she laid on the bed looking around the room, already trying to think how she could get the hell out of there. But she was scared, and all she could think about was her parents and Sam.

CHAPTER 27

Sam felt frantic. "We have to find her. Damn, I knew we should have had more men there. Let's look at all the footage around that area. Do we have any access to any of the satellites in the area?"

"I can check with our contacts and see if they have anything in The Quarter for that area," Les said. "We will get all our team on this. We will find her, Sam."

The team started looking at all cars that had a man and woman in them. They hoped he had not thrown her in the trunk.

"Hey, look at this one from four blocks away. Let's zoom in on that one," one of the officers said.

Sam came over quickly and looked at the photo. He was ready to dismiss the car when he noticed the woman in the passenger seat. Something about her looked familiar. Not the same hair, but her profile looked like Reggie.

"I think that's her," Sam almost yelled. "That bastard gave her a wig. Let's zoom in on the car and see if you can see the plates." Sam noticed Reggie was not hiding her face; in fact, she was looking out the side window at times. He wondered if she knew they would try to find her by the webcams.

The officer working the webcam footage said, "No such luck. This guy is smart. He covered the plates with a decal, probably taking the chance he would not get stopped by the cops. Bet he had an excuse, if stopped, for why they were covered. At least we know it's a small tan compact car with a white stripe on the side. It should not be too hard to find it if we have all the digital files of the highway cams in the system."

Sam did not want to leave the room and kept checking with the team, which had now grown to five people working the computers. There was a team at the coffee shop trying to get prints and information at the same time. They spent hours looking for the car. Finally, they traced it to a particular part of the city.

Sam was feeling hopeful until Paul, one of the team, looked at him and said, his voice lowering, "We lost him."

"What? What do you mean, you lost him?" asked Sam, trying to keep himself from yelling.

"He got to this point and then turned. We can't find another camera yet. Don't worry, we will get this jerk," Paul said.

"Oh shit!" Sam exploded.

"Sam, leave!" Les commanded. "I know you will do this till you find her, but take a five-minute break. Go get something from the hot dog stand, and come back once you have calmed down."

Sam started to protest, but Les said he was not helping by exploding. "Let my guys do their jobs. Go!" Les ordered.

"Okay, but I'll be back soon," Sam said in a low exhausted tone.

Sam went into the break room, sat down at the table, and just put his head in his hands. "Oh, my god, Reggie, please be okay. Please be okay. I am so sorry I did not ask you to marry me before. Oh, my god, Reggie, you can't die."

Sam stayed at the table for a few minutes, then realized this was not going to help Reggie. He got something from the machines, ate it fast, grabbed a cup of coffee, and headed back to the team.

"Okay, I'm back, Les. Anything new?" asked Sam, feeling a bit more level headed and in the game.

"We may have one clue. Looks like the guys checked one of the cameras not too far out of town, and it looks like it could be the one. But again, this guy seems to know where the cameras are." Les rubbed his chin. "We are getting closer. We've decided to put a news bulletin out describing the car and the guy in case anyone knows him. It's a risk, but one we're willing to take."

"I want to man the phones," Sam said. "Somebody must know this guy."

CHAPTER 28

Reggie began to think of all ways she could get out of the room. If The Donation Man had a camera in here, as it seemed he did, she would have to keep away from it or cover where it was recording from. He could be at his work, or who knew where, and still be watching her.

There was no window, except a painting that looked like one, and a small twelve by six inch window at the top of the wall near the ceiling. The vents were small, and the door seemed very heavy, probably made of steel. There were no joints on the door she could slip off to open it. Nothing.

She truly believed Sam would find her, but she was damned if she was going to sit around and do nothing to help herself get out. She began to think of different things she could do if he opened the door. There were no weapons like kitchen knives, lamps, and cleaning supplies. He was smart. Maybe this room had held someone other than her at one time. The house was older, so who knew how long this room had been there?

She tried yelling help over and over again, but nothing.

Suddenly, she heard static and the sound of The Donations Man's voice. "Miss me?"

"Where were you?" Reggie asked. "Please let me out of here!"

"Not for a long time, Reggie. But I am bringing you your dinner. You're not much of a cook, so I figured I would get you some ribs and beans, and maybe if you're good, a can of beer to go with that. There is lots of water in your little refrigerator, so help yourself."

Oh, my god, Reggie thought. *He's treating me like a house guest.*

"Thanks," she said, trying to be convincing.

"I am going to open the opening at the bottom of the door and slide in your dinner. Don't worry, sometime soon you can come out, and we will have a proper dinner at the table. But for now, you just use your desk to eat your meal."

"Can I see the television or call Sam to let him know I am okay?"

The Donation Man roared with laughter. "Call

your boyfriend? You must be kidding me. Sure, let's let him trace the call and find my home."

"Then can you somehow let him know I am okay and alive? Please—"

"No, I won't! You got yourself in this mess. Let him think you are dead. You are never going to see him again anyhow," he said, almost snarling.

"They will find your car. I know it," Reggie said, trying to convince herself.

"Do you think I would be foolish enough to use the same car? I have that hidden in the garage and use my other one. No one is the wiser."

"Oh, God," Reggie moaned to herself.

"Now eat your meal. I have had quite enough of you today. You have annoyed me enough. You will have to have a quiet dinner with no talking. I do have music that can be piped into the intercom, so at least you can have that."

Reggie wanted to yell, "You maniac," but said, trying to sound grateful, "Thank you," instead.

The bottom panel of the door opened, and he slid in a paper plate with ribs and beans on it. She took the ribs and sat at the desk. Her adrenalin flowed as she tried to look calm and relaxed, but her mind was racing about how she could get out of there.

Reggie hovered over her ribs, quickly taking bites, as she was starved. Hoping he didn't see, she let a tiny piece of the bone drop into her lap. Crazy as it seemed, she wondered if she could use it to stab him or hurt him. It was a tiny bone, but maybe she could get him in the eye. Finishing eating, Reggie carefully put the tray on the table, then laid down, slipping the sharp bone under her mattress.

She lay still, trying to think of all the scenarios she could use to get out. She worried about her cat, her parents, Sam, but fatigue overcame her and soon, she was sound asleep.

***

What she did not know was that The Donation Man was in the bedroom outside her door, forming his own plan about what to do with her when they announced on the news that she had been kidnapped. Should he keep her or get rid of her? Probably keep her. No one would know, but time would tell. He thought of the girls he had been with in life, and this one had a certain something about her that he found attractive. Sure, she had been cheap about donating, but still, she had that special something he could live with. He really was not a crazy serial killer as most people would think. He'd only killed one other person, and he did regret that, but he was left with no choice. He had not had a crazy childhood, just an overbearing mother, and now both his parents were dead. No brothers or sisters, or close relatives. Only he did not want to think of that now. Fate had brought him to Reggie with that one call, and who could argue with Fate?

***

Reggie woke up with a start. Her hand brushed roughly against her forehead. "Ouch!" she said as she looked around, trying to get a sense of where she was, when it hit her that she was a captive, she had slept an entire night, and she was still in her clothes.

She heard the sliding of the food drawer and paper plates coming through.

"Wake up sleepyhead," The Donation Man's voice boomed. "I've made an excellent breakfast for you."

Reggie jumped out of bed. "I have to use the bathroom. Don't tell me you have cameras in there too," she said, not being able to keep a little anger out of her voice. "What time is it?"

"Ah, that reminds me, my first gift to you." He slid a small plastic watch thru the small drawer. "Here, Reggie, now you can know what time it is."

Reggie wanted to throw the watch at him, but took it and put it on her wrist.

"Thanks," she said, trying to be submissive sounding.

"No, that is the one place there are no cameras. You can change in there too without worrying I will be watching you."

Reggie was relieved to hear she had some privacy,

and she also had one room that if she could come up with an escape plan, she might be able to figure out something to do in there. Reggie placed the tray on the desk, went quickly into the bathroom, and shut the door. There was no lock, but she was thankful she could close a door.

After she was done, she waited to flush the toilet, trying to see if there was anything in the bathroom she could use against The Donation Man. No mirror. No glass. Only a toothbrush, toothpaste, paper towels, a washcloth, a towel, and a plastic cup. Under the sink, she saw he had put extra toilet paper, tampons, and that was it. She would look more, but she flushed the toilet, washed her hands, and left, knowing this may be a test to see what she would do.

When she came out, The Donation Man was standing in the room. He was carrying his gun, but motioned for her to sit down and eat.

"I am so glad you're here, Reggie. Now sit down and tell me more about your work. I know that you're doing filming here. Tell me about it," he said, almost as if he was her boyfriend or a family member.

Reggie sat down and started eating, not realizing how hungry she was until she smelled the eggs and bacon. He did give her coffee in a plastic cup, but he had made it lukewarm so she could not throw hot coffee at him. Damn, he is careful, she thought, at the same time smiling up at him and beginning to talk about her job. She avoided talking about Jane or her family, or her parents. She'd already seen how he used hurting her friends as a way to get her near him, and she would be devastated if anything happened to her mom and dad.

The Donation Man did not say a word, but seemed to hang on everything she said.

"So what about you?" she asked casually while thinking, so how did you become a psycho?

"There is nothing to say really. I am an only child, born and raised in New Orleans. I have a good paying flexible job, had somewhat normal parents, and have friends, which probably surprises you."

"Where do you work?"

"I don't feel comfortable telling you those things now, Reggie. Someday I will tell you more, but for now, all you need to know is what I told you. Besides, we will be having many meals together when I am not working, so we have time to learn about each other." He gave her a warm smile, and she felt her skin start to crawl as his eyes passed over her body. "You are lovelier in person than you are on camera, Reggie. I know you didn't have any time to bring your clothing, but if you look in the drawers I am sure you will find something that pleases you... or should I say will please me," he smirked. "This also reminds me to tell you that if I will be gone, I will give you two trays, and you can keep something in the mini refrigerator in your room. Don't worry, you'll have good food, Reggie."

The Donation Man got up and took Reggie's tray, all the while letting her know he still had the gun.

"I have got to go to work, but I will stop by later."

"Oh, so you work near here?" Reggie asked, trying to sound casual.

"You really are something." He chuckled and started to walk out the door, his back turned to Reggie.

Big mistake, Reggie thought as she lunged past him. Adrenalin kicked in as she shoved him hard to get past. She was halfway across the bedroom when she felt him slam into her and knock her to the floor. Breathless, Reggie tried to turn over to claw his eyes, but he roughly grabbed her waist and pinned her arms and dragged her back into the room. He didn't say a word, but his eyes were dark with fury as he threw her on the bed.

"You will sit here in the dark with no food while I am gone. If you ever try that again, I will kill you, and slowly." His voice dripped with anger. "I could have shot you, but I didn't, but that doesn't mean you won't pay for this little stunt you pulled," he said, brushing his hand roughly against her breast.

The Donation Man left her in bed and turned out the main light, slamming the door as he left the room. Even the small window did not give the room any light.

Reggie got up with tears in her eyes, sore from his tackle, angry and hopeless, and ran to the door to test the knob. She knew it was locked, but she wanted to see again.

After a few minutes, she heard the startup of his car in the driveway. It was faint, but Reggie had sensitive hearing. He had probably never been in the room alone where she was being held, and had never heard a car leave his driveway.

Score one for me, she thought, clenching her fists *Now I know he is really gone, and I can start my plan. I am not staying in here one more day*, she vowed to herself. *I am strong, I will get him.*

In case he was watching from some remote device, she hobbled into the bathroom to begin her plan, taking the bone from under the mattress with her. She checked the items under the sink and decided she could use the shampoo to blind him, but how would she hurt and catch him off guard without being shot?

She looked around until her eyes focused on the toilet seat. Most toilet seats were bolted down, and this one was no exception. The screws were very sharp, but with the bone she was able to loosen them. If she could use one of them to poke him in the eyes or the carotid artery of his neck, she might have a chance to escape. He had not shut the door when he came in before, as he depended on his gun to get her to stay in the room. She had seen him pull the keys out of his pocket when he was about to leave, so he kept those on him at all times. He also didn't know that after she was shot last year by The Bomber, she had taken martial arts. She was not an expert, but given the right circumstances, and no gun pointing at her, she might be able to hurt him or at least defend herself.

If she could just get outside, Reggie could run and yell, but her first attempt had almost gotten her killed, and left her body sore from his tackling her. But first, how to hurt him, get out of the room, unset the alarm, and run outside? Sadness overcame her at the thought of being killed, not so much for herself, but for how her parents' lives would be ruined, and Sam's, if she died, especially without saying goodbye.

Sticking the screws in her pockets, she went out into the main room without showering or changing, because it would be difficult in the dark, and Reggie did not want to miss him walking in and her chance at surprising him. Her plan could wait a few more days, but if he changed his mind, she could be killed.

Trying to look as calm as she could, Reggie got water from the refrigerator, picked a book from the shelf, and sat down in the chair waiting for The Donation Man's return. It was hard for her to tell what time it was with no lights, except for the window at the top of the room he must have put in to taunt her with the outside world. It was so tiny that even a squirrel could not fit through, but it helped her know it was daylight without using the plastic watch.

Reggie kept listening for the car pulling into the driveway. Luckily the driveway was near this room and not on the other side of the house, which made her wonder if she yelled loud enough a neighbor would hear. Probably not, so she decided to stick to her original plan. By now she prayed Sam would be close to finding her and she would not die.

Looking into the drawer where he said there were clothes, she found sheer nightgowns and sexy clothing. If Reggie didn't die he would keep her locked in this room for his pleasure forever.

Suddenly she heard the sound of a car in the driveway and she went over the plan in her head. Okay, he enters the room. He has a gun. She has the screws, but how to get close enough to get them into his neck and not get shot?

This time he did not slide the meal under the door,

but she heard him unlocking it and stepping into the room. He had his gun, but it was under his belt, and he was not pointing it at her. *Yes!* she thought.

"Hello, Reggie. I got a little time away from my work, so I thought I would come visit," The Donation Man said angrily. "I know you must be bored with only books, being a television reporter, but down the road, once you have proven you can be good, I'll give you a laptop that you can play movies on or watch television. It may upset you, though, if you see the news and every day they wonder what happened to you," he said kindly, yet with a mean quality in his voice at the same time.

"Actually, I love books. I enjoy reading," she said, as if she were talking to a friend she was thanking.

"Here is some more food," he said, turning for an instant to put the bag down on the desk.

Reggie knew it was now or never. Jumping across the room, she ran at him and plunged a screw into his neck. He howled in pain. His eyes turned black as he dropped the gun. He lunged at her, but she kicked him in the groin and he fell to the ground. She tried to kick him again, but he rolled out of the way. When Reggie dove for the gun, The Donation Man grabbed her ankle, causing her to fall and knock the gun under the bed with her hand.

The Donation Man and Reggie struggled around

on the floor. He kept trying to pin her, but she used what she'd learned in martial arts to move out of the different holds he kept trying to put her in. Finally, she got to her feet with him right behind her. She quickly turned around and did a karate punch to the teeth. He howled like a wounded animal, holding his face dripping with blood. Reggie ran by him as he made an attempt to stop her, and ran out of the room, shutting the door behind her.

The Donation Man had the key, but she hoped she could get to the alarm by the front door before he got out and shot her. Running through the bedroom, she slammed that door shut, too. Racing down the hall, Reggie made it to the front door.

She knew four of the five numbers. Quickly keying in the numbers, Reggie tried not to keep looking over her shoulder. She felt her heart might burst out of her chest at any minute.

53042...53142...53242...53342...53442...53542...5 3543...53643...

From behind her, there were the sounds of a door almost being torn from its hinges and a screams of rage.

Oh shit. He got out of the room, she thought. Hearing him opening the bedroom door to the hall, she knew she only had a few seconds. 53742...53842.... Her hands were trembling as she typed in the last possible set of numbers, 53942. Hearing the beep, the green light went on. Pulling her arm back swiftly, she ripped open the door and ran.

A loud gunshot rang through the air, and she felt the sting of a bullet on her right shoulder. "Just go," she told herself. Reggie started screaming, "Help!" She ran into the street, zigzagging to avoid more bullets. Hearing The Donation Man running up fast behind her, she felt sad that she might never see her loved ones again. That thought also made her mad as hell, and she ran faster

Out of nowhere, she saw the flash of lights and a car screech to a stop, and its door busted open. Sam jumped out of the seat. "Get down!" he screamed as he ran by her towards The Donation Man.

Gunshots rang out, and she prayed, "Oh God, don't let anything happen to Sam." She turned to see The Donation Man lying on the ground, blood pouring from his head and Sam standing over him.

The Donation Man weakly sneered at Sam and said, "She will always remember me." With that dying breath, The Donation Man closed his eyes forever.

"Sam!" Reggie screamed as she went to him. "Are you okay?"

Sam didn't say anything. He just held Reggie in his arms as she cried.

After the medics had treated Reggie's wound, all the while with Sam by her side, she asked Sam, "Who the hell was he?"

"We found you by footage of the car," replied Sam. "He never had you cover your face, so I was able to ID you through the window. I'd know your face anywhere. He wasn't so smart. He also put the same sticker on the back of all his cars. It helped us keep an eye on his vehicle." Sam went on and told her The Donation Man had no prior arrests, his coworkers liked him, he had no family alive, or friends it seemed, but his neighbors said he appeared to be a nice guy.

"I'm just glad you found me," Reggie said.

"Me too."

Then they held each other, and lost themselves in each other's eyes as the responders went about clearing the scene.

EPILOGUE:

As Sam and Reggie walked into The Quarter restaurant, there was a round of applause from the room. Jane and her family and Stuart and Annie smiled and clapped. Reggie was only grazed in the shoulder, so she was able to walk without pain.

Reggie felt herself tear up at how lucky she was that she and Sam were standing there together. She started to walk towards the group when she stopped in shock. Her parents were there sitting on the side of the room. They got up and walked towards her and she ran to them, and they all hugged without saying a word.

"Oh Mom and Dad, I am so sorry to have put you through me almost getting killed again. I am so, so sorry!"

Her parents' eyes were teary, and her mom said, "Please, just don't put us through this again, Reggie.

But we are just happy you're alive. What a way for us to visit the city, but we are here. And Sam, thank you!"

"Absolutely. I want to see your daughter alive." Sam chuckled, yet felt this profound sense of relief that Reggie was okay.

As the dinner went on and they all celebrated, Sam pulled Reggie aside and said he wanted to speak to her for a minute. She followed him down the hallway to the restaurant courtyard. Reggie was confused as to why he took her outside, but when he asked her to sit on the bench, she sat down, spreading the skirt of her pale blue dress on the seat.

"Reggie, you know you're the love of my life. Because of you, my days are happier, and I just thank God you're alive. What you don't know is that when I came down this time, I wanted to ask you something."

"What Sam?"

He pulled out a little black box with a ring in it, and got down on his knee beside her and took her hand in his. He flipped opened the box with his thumb, and Reggie gasped. He slipped the ring on her finger.

"I want to spend all the days of my life with you. We have been through rough times together—in fact, almost getting killed twice—but it made me realize that I want to marry you. You are kind, gentle, funny, and I can't imagine spending my life with anyone but you. Reggie, will you marry me?" Sam asked, his voice cracking with emotion.

"Oh, Sam, it is beautiful," Reggie said, holding her hand out and getting teared up herself. She jumped up and wrapped her arms around his neck. "Yes, yes, I want to marry you!" Kissing him over and over, Reggie felt full of life and complete happiness. Then she started laughing and crying all at the same time. "Let's go and tell my parents," Reggie said, barely keeping herself from running in the door.

"Actually, Reggie, they know this is going to happen, as I asked their permission."

"Oh my god, really?" She laughed and asked, "Did they say yes?"

Sam grinned and said, "They were very happy, but I had to promise that we would not make this getting shot once a year a regular thing."

Reggie smiled and touched his cheek lightly. Sam gently held her hand, and they walked into the dining room to tell everyone.

There was a cheer from all at the news, and Reggie looked around at her parents, Stuart and Annie holding hands, and Jane and her family. She was lucky to have such wonderful friends here in New Orleans, her friends back home, and Sam, the one and only Sam — and they were alive.

She smiled as they all raised a glass to toast the future.

Other books by this author:

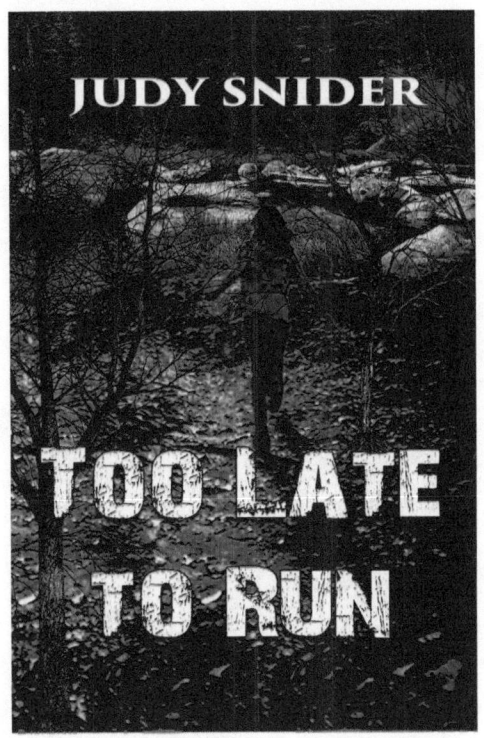

About the Author

Judy Snider lives in Virginia Beach, Virginia with her husband and two cats. She is the mother of two grown sons and has written award winning picture books, one co-authored by her sister. Judy is a retired social worker, a song lyricist and a community volunteer. She was excited to enter the world of writing suspense books with her first suspense novel, Too Late to Run. This is her second suspense novella which has a few of the characters from the book, Too Late to Run. She is working on her third suspense novella, and keeps the reader turning pages to see what will happen next.

To learn more about Judy go to www.judysnider.com

www.ingramcontent.com/pod-product-compliance
Lightning Source LLC
Chambersburg PA
CBHW022114170626
46808CB00002B/719